SKY CHASERS

Emma Carroll

From a prize-winning idea by NEAL JACKSON

Chicken House

2 Palmer Street, Frome, Somerset BA11 1DS
www.chickenhousebooks.com

Text © Emma Carroll 2018
From an original idea by Stephen Neal Jackson
© The Big Idea Competition Limited

First published in Great Britain in 2018
Chicken House
2 Palmer Street
Frome, Somerset BA11 1DS
United Kingdom
www.chickenhousebooks.com

Cover design and interior design by Helen Crawford-White
Cover illustration by David Litchfield
Typeset by Dorchester Typesetting Group Ltd
Printed and bound in Great Britain by CPI Group (UK) Ltd, Croydon CR0 4YY

The paper used in this Chicken House book is made
from wood grown in sustainable forests.

3 5 7 9 10 8 6 4 2

British Library Cataloguing in Publication data available.

ISBN 978-1-910655-53-5
eISBN 978-1-911077-39-8

PRAISE FOR EMMA CARROLL'S BOOKS

Emma Carroll writes original, timeless stories.

THE TIMES

*A deliciously gothic thriller . . . Carroll's story is
skillfully weaved, atmospheric, cinematic and
best read late at night in one sitting.*

THE BOOKSELLER

A gripping adventure . . .

THE GUARDIAN

Absorbing, sensitive and genuinely magical in feel.

THE INDEPENDENT

. . . believable, moving and just the right sort of frightening.

DAILY TELEGRAPH

Emma Carroll is a natural storyteller.

BOOKTRUST

Engaging and entertaining.

INDEPENDENT ON SUNDAY

Destined to be a modern classic in its own right.

IRISH EXAMINER

*This one ticks all the boxes . . .
Emma Carroll is an author to watch.*

BOOKS FOR KEEPS

A MESSAGE FROM CHICKEN HOUSE

I magine a world of dreamers before flying was ordinary . . . how did those dreamers figure out the secret of flight? Inspired by Neal Jackson's original idea – and by history itself! – Emma Carroll reimagines the story of the first ever hot-air balloon. There's fun, underclothes, sheep, Marie Antoinette, spies . . . oh, and a resourceful, clever girl with an intriguing secret. In *Sky Chasers*, Emma brings the quest to life with heartfelt passion – flying has never felt so magical! Hold on tight, folks, and prepare for lift off . . .

BARRY CUNNINGHAM
Publisher
Chicken House

For all those names that
don't make the history books . . .

ONE
FOR SORROW

1

SOUTHERN FRANCE, MARCH 1783

I wait till midnight. On the last chime of the church clock I'm off, flying over the cobblestones on tough-as-leather bare feet. The town, Annonay, lies quiet. Shutters are closed, candles snuffed out. The breath of the place sounds like a person fallen asleep. It's exactly how I want things, just me and the stars and the promise of a few coins for my troubles. They call this part of town 'The Nest', because it's dark and twisty like an animal's lair. Decent, law-abiding folks don't come here. You wouldn't either if you had a choice. Not that the dark scares me – it's daylight that's dangerous when you're a thief.

Tonight though, I'll admit I've got a touch of the nerves. I'm sweating despite it being a cold, March night. All because I've got myself roped into doing a job for someone else — a client, if you will — who cornered me outside the Café Les Ailes at dusk.

'Are you Magpie?' was the woman's opening pitch. She looked me up and down with queer pale eyes like a dog bred for rounding up sheep.

Hand on hip, I stared right back. And what did she make of me, I wondered, a girl with skin browner than most?

'Why? Who's asking?' I said, because I never trust a stranger who knows my name.

'I'm Madame Delacroix. I was told I'd find you here, with your . . . *bird*.' She meant Coco, my tame cockerel who sat, as usual, in the bag I'd made for him, which I wore slung across my chest. 'I'm also told you're the best thief for miles around. If it's true then I'd like you to do a little job for me.'

To be clear, I'm not a hardened criminal — not a murderer or horse stealer. I'm a pickpocket, a finger-smith: a loaf of bread here, a coin or two there. Just enough for me and Coco to get by. I take what rich people are foolish enough to leave unguarded, so the way I see it I'm teaching them a lesson, and there isn't anything criminal in *that*. I've worked by myself, for myself for pretty much as long as I can remember. It's simpler that way.

Yet all she wanted, this Madame Delacroix, was a box fetched from inside a house on the Rue des

Centimes. In her plain black frock, she looked respectable enough, like a governess or a nun, which made me wonder why she couldn't go and fetch the box herself.

'Sorry, lady, I'm not for hire,' I told her.

Which didn't seem to please Madame Delacroix. She had a way of making me feel like she was staring right inside me. I prickled all over. I didn't trust her, I decided, and went to walk away.

'What I'm after is kept inside that valuables box,' she said, a plea creeping into her voice. 'Do at least consider my offer.'

And wouldn't you know it, when she opened her fist – she had gloves on, the leather nice and soft and worth a bit – there were five gold coins sat in her palm. FIVE!

Well of course, I had a sudden change of heart. 'All right,' I said quickly. 'I'll do it.'

She glanced at Coco. 'Without the bird. He'll be too noisy.'

'No, madame, he doesn't make a single sound.' I wasn't lying, either. Since I'd rescued him from a cockfight a few months back, he'd mostly slept and eaten worms and grown new sleek feathers where the old ones'd got ripped out. Never once had I heard him crow.

'Without the bird,' she repeated.

I didn't want to leave him; nor did I want to lose those five gold coins.

So here I am, heading for the river just like Madame Delacroix told me to. I've left Coco tucked under a hedge near the place where I'm to meet her later with the box. Part of me's excited, thinking how, tomorrow morning, I'll actually pay for breakfast. I might even buy a chestnut cake from that fancy pâtisserie called Lancelot's on the Rue Antoine.

It doesn't stop the nerves, though; my hands have gone clammy. And I'm having doubts about those five gold coins. This job must be bigger than I reckoned on – why else would Madame Delacroix pay such a *whopping* amount?

Once I'm over the bridge, I pull a scarf up over my face so only my eyes are on show. I take a deep breath. It's cold tonight, the stars icy-bright, the sky dark as velvet. A clear sky is a good omen. Time for any niggly thoughts to get gone and for me to concentrate.

Take the first flight of steps you come to, Madame Delacroix had said.

I count sixty of them. The steps bring me out on a road that swings sharp left and flattens out. I stop for a quick breather. And to listen. Just to be sure I'm alone.

Once I'm walking again, I start to notice the

houses. In this part of town, they're bigger and grander than the streets I live amongst in the Nest. They've got driveways for carriages, rose gardens, gates. My target isn't the biggest house in the road, nor the smallest. To be honest, I'm surprised at how ordinary it looks next to the others. I'm guessing a family lives here, not that I asked. It's best not to know who you're thieving from. You don't want to get the guilts.

Crouching behind the gatepost, I check: way in? Way out? Dogs? Guards? People still awake? I can't see any signs of life from here.

Once I've got the measure of the place, I slip through the gate. The drive is long, the gravel crunchy underfoot, so I walk on tiptoe until I reach the front of the house. It's deadly quiet, lights out, the glass at the windows black where the shutters haven't been closed. A couple of steps lead up to a side door. This must be the way in. And there it is, the rosemary bush Madame Delacroix mentioned. Her instructions, I admit, are as sharp as you like. It's the perfect spot to crouch down and hide behind, and with a good view of the door.

Yet before I can even reach the bush, the side door opens. I freeze. *Mais non!* This isn't in the plan!

'Hurry up, Voltaire,' says a boy's voice, nudging some sort of animal outside. 'You do your business while I shut the shutters, all right? Be quick!'

A dog. Someone's letting a dog out! In a flash, I drop to the ground.

The boy stays in the doorway. 'What is it, old chap? What've you seen? Is someone there?'

I keep stone still. *Sloppy work, Magpie,* I tell myself, the nerves creeping back, *you've not even got inside and someone's sensed you.*

Yet the dog doesn't bark or growl – it . . . *quacks.* Really, it does. I'm stunned. And overcome with such an urge to laugh, it's a job not to snort, and though I pinch my nose it doesn't help much.

'What've you found, Voltaire?' the boy asks again.

I've got to risk a look. Parting the rosemary branches a little, I glimpse a duck. A real live *duck.* And a fine specimen too – the snowy-feathered kind that roasts up nice and crisp. The boy with it is a solid, healthy sort with dark hair tied back off an honest-looking face. Which again makes me wonder about this job, what his family have done to upset Madame Delacroix. It must be bad for her to hire a thief like me to help put it right.

Silently, I shrink back into the bush. I wait for the boy and his duck to go inside again, then when all is clear, I count to fifty before crawling to the door. It's locked, the key taken, though that's hardly a problem. An old hairpin from my pocket and some fierce concentration should do the trick. With a click, the door opens.

Inside, there's a passage: I follow it deep into the house. The flagstones are smooth, almost warm beneath my feet. I pass through a kitchen where the smell of food – meaty, garlicky – makes my mouth water, though I mustn't let it distract me. I'll grab a handful on the way out if I can.

Upstairs, Madame Delacroix said. *Top of the house. You're looking for a study in the attic.*

Up a flight of stairs, I join another passage, this one carpeted and lit by candles. It seems to run the length of the house. Trouble is, though the doors are all shut, some of them have candlelight leaking underneath. I hear coughing and low voices, which means people are still awake. Not so good. My heartbeat picks up. I can't afford to hang around.

At the end of the passage is the staircase I'm looking for. This one's small and curved, leading up to a second storey – the attic. I'm relieved to find it. The candlelight doesn't reach this far, nor do the voices, so the darkness is oily-thick and silent. I hurry up the stairs.

At the top there's just one door: one room. Even in the dark the quiet feels different; it's the thick, book-muffled kind. I smell leather, candles and ink, and as I creep across the room, paper crunches under my feet.

A valuables box, Madame Delacroix said. *Red leather with gold patterns on it, locks on the front. On the top, the initials: JM.*

Right now though, none of that detail is helpful. It's so dark in here I can't even see my own nose. Nor can I read, so I'll be guessing those initials.

Hands out in front, I feel my way round the room. There's no sign of a box. I'm beginning to lose hope when I jab my toe on something hard. The pain makes me scream – a big silent *waaaaa*! I hop on one foot, rubbing the other.

Then I realize. What I've walked slap-bang into *is* the box. Crouching down, I feel it properly. It's leathery with locks on the front, just as Madame Delacroix said. I grin: I've found it.

No time for congratulations, though. I've got to get this box outside. It's not heavy but it's awkward as heck to carry – it's all sharp corners and too big to sit on my hip. Yet, with the devil's luck and silent footsteps, I'm downstairs in an eye-blink.

As soon as my feet hit the ground floor, I start running. I don't stop for food. Once I get those five gold coins I'm going to buy a whole box of chestnut cakes from Lancelot's.

I'm nearly there. Nearly at the back door. I can already feel an icy draught. It's just down these steps and round this next corner and . . .

I skid to a halt.

The boy and his duck are here, their backs to me, staring at the door.

'I locked it, I'm sure I did,' the boy is saying. 'Good job you wanted to relieve yourself again, Voltaire, or this would've stayed unlocked all night.'

He's suspicious. And I'm panicked. He mustn't see me! Swinging my fist at the lantern just above my head, I knock it to the ground with a crash. The passage goes instantly dark but now there's glass everywhere.

'Stay where you are! Don't move!' The boy sounds more scared than I am.

I rush for where the door should be and go smack into him, catching him off balance.

'Oh no you don't!' the boy cries.

Suddenly, he's holding the other side of the box. I wrap both arms around it, clinging on.

'Let go!' I hiss.

'You let go!' He yanks it towards him. I yank back twice as hard.

There's a *crunch-ping* as the lock on the box's lid springs open. Then the whole thing tips and paper – a right waterfall of it – pours to the floor. I cuss under my breath. *Bring me the whole thing unopened*, Madame Delacroix had instructed.

Well, she'll have to make do, I decide. Letting go of

the box, I grab handfuls of paper, stuffing them down my frock.

'You can't take those!' the boy cries, guessing from the rustlings what I'm doing. 'They're important to us!'

But I need to take something, to prove I've been here. Especially if I want paying. I move faster.

'You mustn't steal them,' the boy pleads. 'I beg of you.'

Someone with a candle comes down the passage towards us. 'What's all this frightful noise?' It's a woman's voice.

I lunge for the door. Like I say, it's not in my nature to dwell on the people I thieve from. All I think now is *run run run*.

2

It's not until I reach the river that I risk a glance behind me. The streets are dark, empty, like they always are this time of night. Once I'm sure no one's followed me I slow to a walk and unwrap the scarf from my face. The papers crackle inside my frock. I *think* I've done all right, but I'm suddenly hit by a bad dose of the doubts. Madame Delacroix wanted the box, didn't she? I've only managed to bring her what was inside. And even then, I didn't get all of the papers.

My mood sinks fast. I'm tired and hungry. I want this job to be finished so I can claim my coins and walk away. If she doesn't give me all five, four would do. Or, if she twisted my arm I suppose I'd take three. Even that's more than I've ever earned before.

The plan is to meet her just past the turnpike. On the left there's a little lane that runs up the valley. At the top of the lane is a gate. That's where Madame Delacroix will be when the clock strikes four. Though I've plenty of time, I'm twitchy to get there because it's where I've left Coco, wrapped in my jacket under a hedge. I don't want the foxes finding him first.

The moon is up, casting shadows as I head out of town. Knowing the sky's above me, clear and bright, I relax a little. A few yards past the turnpike, I take the left turning. It's then I notice footprints in the dirt. One person's. Large. With a delicate, narrow heel.

My shoulders tense. She's early.

The footprints carry on all the way up the lane. It's proper countryside up here with hedges that loom high over your head and the moon is so bright that everything looks silver. Finally, the lane comes to a dead end at a gate. Leaning against it is the outline of a tall, wide-shouldered person, wearing a cape that folds about them like dark wings. Madame Delacroix is waiting for me; it's meant to be the other way round. The change of plan makes me wary as I approach.

'You said four o'clock,' I tell her.

'I've an impatient nature,' she replies, which makes me hope more than ever she's not disappointed with what I've got stuffed down my frock. I notice then

14

she's holding something at arm's length like it's poisonous or vicious.

I stare in horror.

It's Coco. He's still wrapped in my jacket, but scrabbling to get free.

'Don't hurt him!' I cry.

'We've just been getting acquainted, that's all,' she says coolly.

I lick my lips, try to calm down. But my heart's going twenty to the dozen, and I can't keep back. As I go to grab Coco, she twists away, holding him out of reach.

'Now now, it's rude to snatch,' she chides. It's pretty clear she's not going to hand him over, not until I give her what she wants from me. And she can have it, frankly. I'm fed up of the papers prickling my skin.

'Here.' From inside my frock I pull out a fistful. 'Take 'em.'

In one quick movement I seize the bundle of Coco and my jacket and thrust the papers into her hand. It takes her by surprise. She lets go, then looks down at the papers. 'What the deuce are *these*?'

'The box was too awkward.' I try to explain. 'I couldn't keep hold of it. And it was risky. At the house, people were still awake.'

She narrows his eyes at me. 'Who, exactly?'

I think of the boy and his duck at the back door,

the woman with the candle coming down the passage. Decent folk who I don't want to dwell on. 'I don't know who—'

She interrupts. 'I sent you to take a valuables box from a house. It was quite simple. You said you could do it. You're supposed to be the best.'

I start to get angry. 'Now look here, lady, I did what I could. The box was full of these papers. I thought you wanted them.' I pull out the rest from my frock, but she slaps my hand away and it all flutters to the ground.

'What have I ever wanted with *papers*?' she cries.

'But they—'

'That family you've just visited,' she talks over me, '*own* the big paper mill on the outskirts of town. Paper, for them, is like air, so don't pretend you've brought me something of worth.'

'But these ones were locked away,' I insist. 'Mightn't that mean they're valuable?'

This gets her attention. With an irritable sigh, she picks up a handful of papers from the ground and starts to shuffle through them. I watch her. At first, she looks almost bored. My heart sinks. I stroke Coco's head to steady myself.

Then she does another sigh, this one's a sharp breath in. She sounds startled. Excited, even. A slow smile creeps over her face.

16

'Well, well,' she murmurs, reaching for more papers. 'Someone's been rather busy.'

I don't know what she means. I keep watching, though. She's frowning now, chewing on the inside of her cheek, thinking fast. And I'll admit I'm a tiny bit pleased. Such a fuss and she's found something valuable, after all. I did right to grab the papers.

As she carries on reading, I reach under the hedge for Coco's sling-bag; it's still there where I left it earlier. I slip him inside. It's time we were gone.

'Did you get *all* the papers?' she asks suddenly.

'Most of them.' Giving my hand a quick wipe on my skirt, I hold it out. 'You going pay me, then?'

There's a beat when she looks down at the papers again. Then she lunges at me. It catches me off guard.

'Hey! What're you—'

She's got me by the throat, squeezing, pushing. The leathery creak of her gloves. Long fingers like vines slither right round my neck. I can't breathe.

'Money?' she hisses. 'You've got a nerve! The job's not finished, not by a long shot.'

I try to speak but she's holding me too tight. I'm furious at being caught out. Number one rule of the streets: what you lack in muscle, you make up for in speed. I can run like a greyhound, but I'm no match for a well-fed, full-grown woman, though I scratch and kick all the same.

17

'I'd kill you if I thought someone might actually miss you,' she tells me.

I'm panicking. I think she's going to kill me anyway. My head's ringing. Everything starts to look gold and powdery. Across my chest, I feel Coco scrabbling to get free of the sling.

'Arggh!' Madame Delacroix cries. 'That wretched bird's bitten me!'

Just like that, she lets go of my throat, shoving me so hard I trip over my own feet. I land on the ground with a thud. There's not enough air to breathe even though I'm gulping it down. When I look up, eyes streaming, she's there, standing over me. There's blood on her face. Wrapping my arms round Coco, I try to soothe him. I'm as scared as I've ever been.

'You listen to me, you worthless little scrap,' she spits. 'This job isn't finished until I've got that box.'

My mouth drops: oh blimey, she wants me to go back in to the house.

She must see my shock because she leans right in till she's way too close. 'We'll talk again, Magpie.'

Then she steps over me like I'm horse dung in the road. I don't call out. Don't move. I listen to the swish of her skirts through the grass. The sound gets fainter, until it's gone – *she's* gone. Once I'm sure, I roll onto my side, coughing till I'm sick.

I do sit up eventually. The warmth of Coco's little

body makes me feel a bit better.

'You saw her off, didn't you boy?' I tell him. 'You fought better than me.' Though I've no idea what I'm going to do next because Madame Delacroix will be back, I know she will.

Scattered across the grass lie the not-good-enough papers. The damp's already got to them, making them limp like cloth. Half-heartedly, I prod at a couple of pieces with my foot.

All right, so I didn't get the box she wanted. But she *was* intrigued by these papers, wasn't she? And didn't she ask if there were any more?

I'm confused. Tired. My neck hurts where she grabbed me. But still I crawl over to the papers for a better look. The moon's bright enough to see the funny whiskery writing on them, and pictures. Lots of pictures.

The writing makes no sense to me, but the pictures do. There's the sky, a group of trees, some hills. Then another of rooftops and church spires. Another one is all stars.

I like them. *Really* like them, I mean. They're messy, like someone's drawn them in a hurry, their ideas coming so fast they can hardly keep up. In each picture is a shape – a sort of oblong. It might be the way I'm looking at it, but it's as if it's hanging in the sky. It can't be though. Only birds and dreamers get to fly.

TWO
FOR JOY

3

The next thing I know, it's morning. The weather's changed so it's a different sort of day – blustery, warmer, though I'm stiff and cold from not sleeping, thinking all night about that blasted box and the drawings inside. We haven't budged from the lane yet. Last night it felt safer to stay put than to follow Madame Delacroix back into town. At some point Coco and I snuggled down under a hedge, and that's where we are now, my rooster still asleep in the crook of my arm. He's not an early riser or a crower. Sometimes, I think he's more pet dog than poultry.

Yet when I wriggle out from the hedge, there's no paper in sight. Not a single sheet. The wind's taken it all, I suppose, which means it could be anywhere. I don't know if I'm dismayed or relieved.

The sky at least is a comfort. It's my favourite type – breezy-blue with clouds moving fast across it – and just seeing it clears my head. I'm feeling braver today. That nasty woman can find someone else to fetch her box, I decide. Next time she comes asking, I'll tell her where to stick it.

I'm leaning on the gate, mulling this over, when I spot something odd in the sky. It's directly up ahead, above a group of trees. I honestly think I'm so tired and needing to eat that my eyes are playing tricks. As the thing floats closer, I can see it's white. Oblong-shaped. Not a cloud. *Definitely* not a cloud. It isn't a kite. Or a bird, either. I'm itching to follow it.

Grabbing a sleepy Coco, I put him in his sling and go through the gate. The field beyond is huge, full of scrubby-brown grass that runs all the way down the hill back towards town. Away from the shelter of the hedge, I'm struck by how strong the wind is. My skirt gets flattened against my legs. I can't stand upright without rocking back on my heels. About thirty feet up, the white object is racing along. It looks like a giant sheet blown free of its laundry line.

Suddenly, a man's voice: 'Grab a rope! For good-ness' sake don't let go!'

It startles me. Though there's not a living soul in sight, the speaker sounds too close for my liking. I'd rather not be seen, not up here in a field in the early morning. It looks suspicious. Best thing is to keep still and crouch down.

'Oh Papa, can't we let it fly?' a younger voice replies. 'It's never travelled this far before!'

The two of them appear from the hedgerow, striking out across the field from a spot not far from me. All I see is their back view – a man in tatty wig wearing a green coat, and a boy with him, dark-haired and excitable. They're running straight for the flying object. Not halfway down the field, the man stops, holding his side like he's got a stitch. 'Go after it! Grab it!' he yells to the boy.

I watch with interest. Out in the open, it's easier to see what's wrong – there are ropes dangling from the object but no one's holding on to them, so it's fast drifting away.

A decent thieving gives you a buzz, yet this is something else. Where's the contraption going to end up – the next field? The river? The next town?

The boy keeps running. But he's heavy-footed and clumsy, and can't quite catch it. At last, with a bit of luck, he manages to grab one of the ropes. And just in time. A sharp gust of wind sends the object swooping upwards, twisting and dancing.

The boy holds on tight. His legs are splayed like he's trying to make himself heavier and steadier. But he's no match for the wind. The object is moving so fast it starts dragging him along the ground, back up the field.

The boy cries out. 'I can't, Papa! I can't . . .' He's shouting something about a knot around his wrist. Though I don't get the exact words, I hear his terror. Now I'm starting to worry too.

'Hold on, son! Just hold on!' the older man tells him.

There's a blast of wind, so strong it sounds like it's tearing the object as it comes, bumping and twisting over the grass. The man tries to reach one of the trailing ropes. He lunges, arms out. Misses.

Another great gust. This time the shape rises higher, taking the boy with it. I watch, open-mouthed, as his feet lift off the ground. He lands, bounces, takes off again. I sense in the pit of my stomach that this isn't meant to be happening. The boy starts to scream.

I don't even stop to think. I run as fast as I can towards the ropes. As I reach the man, he's startled to see another person here, but waves me on.

'Go after him! You'll be faster than me,' he gasps.

I nod. 'Hold my rooster, will you?'

The man's eyebrows shoot up.

'Just mind you look after him.' I say, putting Coco very firmly in his arms.

Within moments, I've caught up with the boy – or rather, his feet, which hang close to my head. There's a lull in the wind. As the flying object drops a little, so does he, though he can't let go of the rope because it's tied too tight.

'Don't kick me.' I warn him. 'I'm trying to help.'

He stares at me, bewildered. Funny, but his face – dark-featured, kind – looks somehow familiar. With a jolt, I realize I *know* him. This is *not* good news. In fact, I'm cringing. Because he's the boy from the house last night, who had the pet duck, who caught me red-handed with the box.

I've no idea if he recognizes me without my face scarf. I dearly hope not. Besides, there's no time for pleasantries. The wind is rising again; I can hear it in the trees.

'Get ready.' I say. 'Two of us might be able to control this thing if we're quick.'

We aren't quick enough.

With a roaring sound, the bag-like structure fills with air. It rises straight upwards, the boy still attached. The force of it tears the rope from my hands.

'Hang on!' I cry. 'Don't let go!' Though he can't do much else with that blasted knot still in place. Off across the field he goes, dipping and bumping with the wind. I race after him. We cross another field. Go over hedges. Across a lane. My legs will hardly keep going when – finally – in the middle of a ploughed field, the whole contraption sinks to the ground. The boy's feet touch down beside it. I come to a panting halt in front of him.

'It'll go up again once the wind starts,' I gasp. 'For pity's sake loosen that knot.'

'I daren't,' he replies. 'If it flies off without me we'll lose the prototype.'

'And you'll be lost too,' I tell him. I don't ask what a prototype is.

But it's like he's seized up with fear. So I start on the knot myself, and manage to work it loose. All the time, the wind stirs my hair.

The fabric begins to swell once more. With a great *whoosh*, it's upright again. The boy cries out, tries to keep his footing. But as the object lifts off, he's stumbling and running after it. I make a desperate grab for his coat. His legs. Any part of him.

From behind me, comes a shout, 'For heaven's sake, get one of the other ropes!'

As a fat length of rope trails past, I grip hold with all my might. Now I'm being dragged too. My feet are on the ground still, but only because my legs are going like windmills to keep up.

All at once the ground falls away. We lift up. And up again. My stomach goes skywards. I'm running on air. The rope gives a short, sharp jerk. All I can do is hold on tight.

The boy can't manage it though. My heart beats in

my mouth as, very slowly, he lets go. He doesn't make a sound as he falls. I squeeze my eyes shut. I can't look.

But the urge to know he's all right takes over. Peering down, I see he's landed on the grass some ten feet below.

'Say something, son.' The man, his voice oddly clear, bends over him. 'Does anything hurt?'

'It all hurts. Honestly, Papa, I'm never doing that again, so don't ask.' The boy – his son – manages to sit. Then he notices me. 'Look at the girl! Look!'

They gaze up at me, wonder in their faces. It's funny: no one's ever looked at me like that before. Soon though, I've left them behind.

Without the boy's weight the bag keeps rising. I go over another field, another lane with cattle walking along it. I clear a barn roof. Go higher still. The muscles in my arms are burning. I can't hold on much longer. And I know falling from this height would more than hurt. The ground would rush up to meet me and then . . . *THUD*. I'd be dead. All I can do is pray it'll be swift.

Thinking like this, I begin to feel almost calm. If these are to be my last moments on earth, I'm not going to miss a second of it. The view from up here is magnificent.

Though my arms ache more than ever, I'm getting used to that bobbing, weightless feeling. I can't believe

I'm *flying*. Time and again I've looked up at the sky and wished myself there. Or envied pigeons pecking in the gutter for being able, with a flap of their wings, to escape the filthy streets. And now it's happening to me. I feel lighter. Like my body doesn't matter. For once I'm not cold or hungry. I'm brave and strong and alive.

The world from up here *looks* different, too, like a toyshop window, or as if a magic spell has been cast across the land. Everything's smaller. Sweeter. Cows in the fields are little bits of china. The river flowing out of town is mirrored glass. Passing over prickly looking treetops makes me think of artichokes. And I'm a bird, looking down on it all, wondering if I'll ever grow bored of the view.

I don't get the chance.

The wind drops suddenly. What, seconds ago, was a plump shape above my head now collapses with speed. The trees loom closer. Within moments, my feet touch the topmost branches. The bag flops, lifeless, beside me. The branches creak at my weight. Something beneath me snaps and down I go.

I fall slowly. Like a feather – only nowhere near as graceful because my hair, clothes, skin snag and tear as I drop through the branches.

I hit the ground with an almighty thud. The air whooshes from my chest. Everything feels wrong. I don't know what part of me to move first. When I try to sit up, my left shoulder makes a crunching, popping sound. I don't scream. But I feel a cold, shivery sweat breaking out across my back. Above me, the trees are curving inwards. It gets darker. The last thing I see are two sets of white-stockinged legs running towards me.

4

I'm pretty certain I've died and gone to that paradise place in the sky. Though I don't much mind *where* I am — it's so warm and comfy here — just as long as no one asks me to move. When I open my eyes, though, I see sheets and blankets, a pillow squished under my head. For the first time in my life, I'm lying in a proper bed.

The kind-faced boy is here with me. He's sitting beside my bed, reading, his pet duck perched on the back of his chair. The duck's the first to spot I'm awake, and I swear he gives me the evils, like he doesn't trust me an inch. I stare back at him, the stupid duck, which makes him quack crossly.

This gets the boy's attention. As he looks up from his book, he smiles. '*Bonjour!* How are you feeling?'

I try to shuffle up the bed; it isn't easy because my left arm's been strapped across my chest. It hurts, too – everything does, like a bull's stomped over me, then turned around and done the whole thing again.

'I'll live.' I'm not exactly used to beds or being asked how I am, and feel a bit awkward. 'Where are we?'

'My house – I mean, my parents' house. We brought you back here after the accident. Don't you remember?'

I shake my head. Everything's blurry round the edges still. I remember flashes of things – the view from up in the air, the popping noise my shoulder made. And something shadowy that I can't quite get hold of, that makes my stomach turn with dread.

'What's your name?' the boy asks. 'I'm Pierre Montgolfier. And this –' he turns to tickle the duck under its beak, '– is Voltaire, my pet duck.'

'Big name for a duck,' I remark.

Pierre grins. 'Isn't it? I named him after the writer, you know.'

I don't. But I remember hearing from somewhere about Pierre's lot owning the paper mill, which means they're not short of a coin or two, so he obviously reads and writes and does clever things.

'What's your name?' Pierre asks.

'Umm . . .' I'm thinking it might be simpler to

make something up. But Pierre's face is kind: I like it.

'I'm Magpie,' I say.

'Magpie? Is that a girl's name?'

I bristle a bit. 'Well, it's *my* name, if that's what you mean.'

'And your family name?'

I blink. *A family name?*

'I don't have a family. It's just me and Coco,' I reply.

I could tell Pierre that my father came from Algiers on a stolen boat, that I've got his dark skin and hair and taste for adventure. My mother had tastes of a different sort: she drank gin and died of it when I was barely old enough to remember. From then on, I had to fend for myself. And I did all right at it too. Families, I reckon, are over-rated.

'Magpie,' I repeat, firmly. 'I'm Magpie. How long have I been here?'

Pierre counts on his fingers. 'Two weeks and a day . . . no, two days.'

I'm horrified. '*Really?*'

But I never stay longer than a single night anywhere. A new night, a new doorway, that's my motto. It's safer that way. If you keep moving, nothing – or no one – catches up with you.

'Have I been asleep all that time?' I ask.

'Pretty much, yes. You said some funny things in your sleep, too, something about gold coins and the deal being done? Does that mean anything to you?'

I shake my head. Yet the feeling of dread grows stronger. Just around the corner of what I can remember is someone I'd rather not meet again. If it's known I'm here, they'll come looking for me and I don't wish any trouble on Pierre's family.

'Well ta for everything, but I'd better be off,' I say, swinging my legs over the side of the bed.

I try to stand but the floor has other plans. It tilts like a ship in a storm, making me drop down onto the bed again.

'Nice try,' Pierre says. 'You're not going anywhere until you're better.'

'I *am* better,' I protest. 'It's decent of your family to take me in and all, but just tell me what you've done with my rooster and we'll be on our way.'

'That bird you gave to Papa? The one that sleeps all the time?' Pierre asks. 'He followed us home. We can't get rid of him.'

'Is he all right?'

Pierre nods. 'He's been waiting outside your bedroom door all this time. He's pining for you, Magpie.'

Poor Coco. I'm almost teary. 'Can I see him?'

Pierre opens the door. And there, just outside, is my dear orange-feathered friend. If a rooster's face could fill with joy, his does just that. Before Pierre can even catch him, he's dashed into the room and up onto the bed, where he settles into the crook of my good arm like we've never been apart. Instantly, I'm feeling better, and try again to get out of bed, but still don't manage it.

'Stop being so stubborn. You need to rest,' Pierre tells me. 'You fell a long way that day, helping us with our prototype.'

That funny word again.

It jogs my memory some more, and slowly, bit by bit, the fog inside my head begins to clear. Now I can picture ropes trailing along the ground. The wind was too strong for us, wasn't it, the white object filled up with too much air or . . . or . . . something . . . and it was moving too fast, and lifting away from the ground.

But it isn't the falling part I remember most. It's the bit before – the flying part – that comes back to me the strongest. The field slipping away from me, the look of wonder on Pierre and his father's faces. It was the most incredible, magical thing that's ever happened to me. My heart thumps just from thinking about it.

'I'd help again, too, honest I would,' I say. 'Shame you fell when you did because it was *fantastic* up there in the air. You'd love it.'

'Believe me, I wouldn't,' Pierre replies. 'No one was

meant to fly that day, and I've no plans to repeat the experience. It's completely unsafe.'

'Maybe one day it will be, though.'

He quickly changes the subject. 'I don't mean to be rude Magpie, but you smell like an old donkey. No, actually, *worse* than an old donkey.'

'Well, *you* smell like . . .' The truth is he's so clean he doesn't smell of anything.

Half an hour later, a sullen-faced servant girl arrives. She's sweating under her arms and down her back like she's got a fever – no wonder when I see the tin bath she's dragging behind her.

'Brought this all the way up from the basement so you'd better be grateful,' she says, scowling at me.

Dumping the bath, she disappears, returning again and again with jugs of hot water until it's filled. On one of these trips she forgets to shut the door and I overhear her talking in the passageway.

'I'm carrying this bathwater and can't do nothing else, Madame Verte,' she complains. 'There's the animals to feed and Monsieur Joseph's gone all strange – one minute he wants his pencils sharpened, the next he's shouting and screwing up paper and saying he can't make his designs work any more.'

'It's this obsession with flying, Odette,' replies an older woman. 'Ever since his notes disappeared that night he's more or less given up. But he won't go back to working at the mill. He just sits up in his study all day, staring out of the window.'

My ears prick at this. Missing notes? Sounds familiar.

And the final bit of the puzzle comes to me, *click, clunk*, like opening a lock with a hairpin. Which was exactly how I broke in here that night, wasn't it, though I'm not proud of it now. In fact, I'm out and out ashamed. Those papers I took – the different skies, the object floating in each one – were designs for Pierre's father's flying creation, weren't they?

I groan miserably. I've done a shoddy thing, even by my usual low standards.

Odette's talking again: 'I reckon it's the accident. Never mind what happened to that Magpie – from what I've heard, Pierre nearly came a cropper, too.'

'Can't risk losing the only son, can they?' Madame Verte agrees.

'Only *child* by the way Madame Montgolfier's been recently. She don't need anything else to fret about, that's for sure.'

When Odette stomps back into the room, I try to make it look like I've not been listening. She hands me a lump of something wrapped in paper. I sniff it warily.

'It's soap.' She stares in disbelief. From her apron

pocket, she produces a pair of shears and comes at me with them.

Horrified, I shrink back into the pillows. 'What are those for?'

'Your hair. Madame Verte says it's to come off. You've got lice.'

'I haven't.' But I'm instantly scratching my head. I'm crawling with lice, of course I am.

She makes me get out of bed and sit on an upright chair. She isn't gentle with the shears, either. Soon the floor's covered in so much hair I can't imagine there's any left on my head. With a look of disgust, she sweeps it into a bucket for burning.

I'm wearing a nightgown-type slip, the sleeves of which roll up easily so Odette can take the strapping off my bad arm. Before I know it, she's whipped the nightgown off too. And I'm stood there, starkers and shivering.

'No looking,' I warn her.

She rolls her eyes. 'I've got better things to gawp at than your scrawny body.'

By now, though, I'm almost glad to get into the bath. It feels like sitting in a giant, lukewarm puddle, and that's the nice bit. When Odette scrubs my back I'm sure she's mistaken me for a stone floor.

Afterwards, she gives me a clean nightgown. The bath has left me so wobbly-weak I'm glad to get back into bed. Right on cue, Voltaire the duck's head appears round the door, then Pierre's.

'You look better.' He grins. 'Can we come in now?'

I give a weary shrug. I suppose boys like him, and their ducks, don't have much else to do all day. Taking the seat by the bed again, Pierre passes me a little mirror, the sort that'd make a few coins for its silver. 'Have you seen yourself?'

Reluctantly, I take the mirror. I've seen enough of my reflection in shop windows and horse troughs to know I'm no beauty. Still, it comes as a shock to see myself without hair. Don't think I'm vain, but my eyes look way too big and my freckles stand out like tea-leaves on my cheeks. I'm all sharpness and shadows. I thrust the mirror back at Pierre.

'I look like a boy,' I mutter, hugging Coco to me. At least he doesn't seem to mind. Yet Voltaire, who's sat importantly on Pierre's knee, quacks. 'See, even your duck thinks so.'

'You look better than you did before,' Pierre remarks.

I tense up: what *before* does he mean? *Before* the bath? *Before*, downstairs by the back door when I tried to steal the box? What if the scarf round my face didn't fool him? Does that mean he knows who I am?

Once again, I get the feeling that this bedroom – this lovely, comfortable bedroom – is a trap.

40

'I'm not under arrest, am I?' I ask nervously.

'Arrest?' Pierre frowns. Thinks about it. 'Well, I suppose that rather depends on what you are.'

'What *I am*?'

'All that talk of gold coins in your sleep. You could be a spy, working for someone.'

I cough back a laugh. 'A *spy*?' He's definitely been reading too many books. But at least he doesn't seem to think I'm a thief, and I'm glad. I've never cared for people's good opinions before, but Pierre's somehow seems to matter.

'I mean it,' Pierre says. 'There *are* spies out there. We've had one break in here already recently, which made us realize the threat is real, though thankfully the papers stolen weren't too vital.'

'Really?' My voice is a strangled squeak. 'That's ... um ... shocking.'

Heat spreads across my neck: I yank the covers up to hide it. I might as well have a big 'guilty' sign hanging over my head.

Amazingly, Pierre doesn't seem to notice.

'It was, Magpie. So we have to be doubly careful from now on,' he explains, because he's far too nice to think I might not be on his side.

And I have to admit, this talk of spies is intriguing. I wriggle up into a half-sitting position. 'What're they after, these spies?'

'Knowledge,' Pierre replies. 'We're not the only ones trying to invent a way to fly, you know. There's a race on. And no one wants to be second.'

'Who're they working for?'

'The English.' Pierre blows out a sigh. 'Though they're not having much more luck than us, by the sounds of things. They can't keep their structure inflated, either. Nor have they worked out the weight issue.'

I frown. 'Weight issue?'

'How much the structure can tolerate, so it's able to get off the ground for a decent flight, but isn't at the complete mercy of the weather.'

'The wind, you mean?' I say, thinking how the object had been tossed about like a scrap of paper.

'Exactly.'

'So the English are trying to steal your ideas, are they?'

'I know they are, Magpie. I've seen them. Spies are easy enough to spot if you know the signs.'

'Go on, then.' I'm trying not to smile. 'How d'you spot a spy?'

'People acting out of place. Who let slip information that they couldn't possibly know. Or . . .' Pierre raises an eyebrow, ' . . . who sneak about in the middle of the night.'

'Right. I see.' I'm serious again. This spying lark

sounds a lot like thieving. It's taking something that's not yours.

Though part of me thinks it sounds a bit far-fetched, I honestly can't forget what it felt like to fly. And like anything in this life that's worth something, it's not long before other people start circling, sniffing, wanting it for themselves. A thief like me knows that all too well.

5

Another few days and I'm well enough to get up properly. First thing I do is open the window, breathing in all the early morning I can get. Today's sky is a beauty, pale blue and pink-flecked, the kind that promises another fine Annonay spring day. These weeks of being indoors have softened me up. I'm slower, sleepier, which is no good if you count on sharp wits to get by. Funny too how not being hungry all the time gives you a chance to think about other things – like flying, and how that object might've stayed longer in the air. Not that it's my concern. I've poked my nose around here too much already.

Something down by the orchard catches my eye. It's under the trees. A grey shape that's there, then gone again. A shadow, probably, though it makes me suddenly afraid. I try not to think it's Madame Delacroix, though I bet it won't be long before our paths cross again.

Then Pierre arrives in a whirlwind of curly hair and coat-tails. Voltaire has to waddle fast to keep up.

'*Vite*, Magpie!' Pierre cries. 'Papa's asked to see you.'

I'm taken aback. 'What for?'

'I don't know. But you're to call him Monsieur Joseph, and wear these.' He thrusts a bundle of clothes at me. 'You are well enough, aren't you?'

'I think so.' I'm actually glad of the distraction. 'Look away then, while I get dressed.'

As Pierre turns around, I shake out the frock he's given me. It's like the ones Odette the servant wears, with a muslin cap to match: I don't fancy myself in it much.

'Where's my own stuff?' I ask. I'd a perfectly decent frock on when I'd got here. 'Can't I wear that?'

Pierre glances down at Voltaire: 'Will you tell her, or shall I?'

The duck quacks; it sounds like a rude word, and I can't help sniggering.

Pierre, though, keeps a very straight face. 'Your old dress had lice in it, that's what Voltaire's trying to tell you. And it was rotten under the arms.'

'Rubbish!' I tell him. 'That was my best dress.'

It was my only one, too.

The study looks different in daylight. Above our heads are three attic windows, each one full of sky: no wonder Monsieur Joseph spends his time staring out of them. Everything else – the papers, the books, the mess of the place – is just as I remembered, and it makes me both edgy and at ease. The man sitting at the desk I recognize as Pierre's father. From the strain on his waistcoat buttons, I'd say he's done more eating than running across fields recently. Despite all the mess around him, his desk is completely clear: no pens, no pencils, no paper, no notebooks. He's obviously not working, Odette and Madame Verte were right. All over again I feel bad about the papers, because he needs them more than I ever did. My guilts aren't helped by seeing the red valuables box on a nearby shelf, though I try not to stare.

'The duck waits outside,' Monsieur Joseph says. He clicks his fingers at Voltaire, who shakes his tail feathers in disgust.

'Oh Papa,' Pierre pleads. 'You know how he likes to feel included.'

Monsieur Joseph sighs and sits back in his seat. 'He also has a habit of pooping all over the place.'

I catch Pierre's eye: he pretends to look annoyed but does as his father asks. Then it's our turn for a

46

finger-click as we're directed to sit in two chairs. Both are piled high with books that we have to move first.

'What work do you do, Magpie?' Monsieur Joseph asks.

'Ummm . . .' I'm unsure how to put it. He's got the same kind face as Pierre, only older, more worried-looking. But I don't suppose he'd want to hear the truth.

'I'll cut to the point,' he says. 'Our housekeeper Madame Verte insists we need extra help now my brother is living with us. My wife, Madame Mont-golfier, is unwell currently, which also puts a strain on things.'

Odette was gossiping about this out in the corridor, wasn't she? I feel bad all over again for not being more grateful to her. With one sick person in the house already, nursing me was extra work she didn't need.

'So,' Monsieur Joseph continues. 'Pierre thinks the position may suit you. Would you be interested?'

I puff my cheeks in surprise. *Me*, work here, at the Montgolfiers' house? After I'd stolen his papers?

He doesn't know that thief was me, though. He just thinks I'm the girl who had the nerve to keep hold of his flying machine. I'm the girl who went up into the sky. And, you know what, I reckon I could get used to being *her*, even if does mean I'll have to dress like Odette.

47

'Or are you expected somewhere else?' Monsieur Joseph asks.

I think briefly of the shadow I saw under the trees.

'No Monsieur, I'm not expected,' I reply.

'*Bon*. You'll start work as soon as you're able.' He peers at me properly. '*Are* you able? Has your shoulder healed enough?'

''Course,' I say quickly, before he thinks I'm not up to it.

'Now Papa,' Pierre steps in. 'While we're here, why don't you ask Magpie about her experience of flying?'

I grin — I can't help it — because I've been hoping he might ask, and truth be known, I'm dying to talk it over. But Monsieur Joseph looks suddenly uncomfortable. 'Pierre, I really don't think—'

'You should listen to her,' Pierre cuts in. 'It might help you start working again.'

'My work is well enough — it needs no help,' Monsieur Joseph mutters, with a shifty cough.

He's lying.

Pierre rolls his eyes. 'Papa, admit it. You're stuck. You've done nothing since the day we brought Magpie here.'

'Since the accident, you mean?' Monsieur Joseph says with some force. 'Our little experiment didn't go well that day, did it? You've clearly forgotten that you and Magpie nearly died.'

Pierre flinches. 'Of course I haven't! I'm still having nightmares about it, but that doesn't mean you should stop—'

'Your dear mother would never forgive me if anything happened to you. Goodness knows, in her frail state she'd probably not survive the shock. No, I've decided. It's simply too dangerous.'

'Papa, I think you should—'

'The design was never right,' Monsieur Joseph interrupts again. 'We've suffered so many setbacks it's wiser to cut our losses. We shouldn't waste any more time and effort on something that's doomed to fail.'

They both go quiet. Pierre stares at his feet, Monsieur Joseph at the wall. I know that if I don't say something now I'll regret it. Because one of those *setbacks* was my fault and if Monsieur Joseph could just hear, for a minute, what it felt like to be up in the air, then he'd know it was worth every tiny second, every risk.

'Umm . . . Monsieur, that day in the field,' I stumble to find the right words, 'with the . . . ummm . . .'

'. . . The prototype,' Pierre nods in encouragement. 'Go on, keep talking. Tell him what it was like to fly.'

'You flew too,' I remind him. 'What did you think of it?'

His face pales. 'It was awful. Terrifying. But you—'

'I loved it.' I finish for him. 'It was incredible. If

there was a way of making it steadier, and having some sort of control over the going up bit, then you could stay up in the air, well, for *hours*!'

Monsieur Joseph holds up his hand like he wants me to stop. But it's all bubbling up inside of me, though I'm struggling to explain it.

'It was like that curtain,' I point to the open window behind him. 'The wind lifts it, fills it up, then lets it fall.'

At least now Monsieur Joseph turns to have a look.

'Yes, Monsieur,' I tell him. 'It only went upwards when the wind got . . . I don't know . . . inside of it somehow. It made it bigger. Fuller . . .'

'Hmmm . . .' Monsieur Joseph mutters. 'That might make sense . . .'

He's beginning to consider me more seriously. Pierre nudges his father. 'Shouldn't you be writing this down?'

But Monsieur Joseph sits back in his seat, spreading his hands wide on the desk.

'Let me be clear. You believe that our contraption only gained height with air *inside* the bag.'

'Yes.'

'Yet once the air seeped out again, height was quickly lost . . .' He stops. Looks suddenly very intense. 'Were you alone that day, Magpie? It's important our prototype stays an absolute secret. If any of

50

what happened gets out—'

'I'm not a spy, if that's what you mean,' I say, sharp as you like.

The study door swings open. In strides a man I've never seen before, so tall and wide and strong as a tree that everything else in the room seems to shrink, me included.

'Who's he?' I mouth to Pierre.

'My uncle, Monsieur Etienne, Papa's brother,' he whispers and pulls a face.

'You're quizzing our *guest*, I see,' Monsieur Etienne says, his gaze sliding over me.

I give him a quick once-over too but can't find the family resemblance. There's no kind face here, no worried brow. This Montgolfier's all swagger and confidence. I bet he'd not give up on the prototype so fast, either.

'Magpie's just been sharing her account of the flight,' Monsieur Joseph explains. 'I confess it's worth hearing.'

I'm ready to keep going, but Monsieur Etienne tuts irritably. 'I realize girls can be clever, dear brother, but with all due respect, girls like Magpie don't even have an education. Let's not involve her in the finer details of our invention, eh?'

It's true: I can't read or write. But I'm far from stupid. Though I haven't got a gob full of fancy words to describe what happened that day, I was there. I *was* part of it. And I've a few more 'finer details' to share.

'It was the wind that kept your air bag moving,' I say, before he can stop me. 'You'll need to weigh it down a bit to give it more direction. Get the weight right and it'll go higher and be more steady.'

I see the look Monsieur Etienne gives Monsieur Joseph. It's frustrating but I keep going.

'Think about it,' I tell them. 'When it was me and Pierre hanging on, it only went so high. Then when he . . .'

'Fell off.' Pierre grimaces.

'. . . well, on my own I travelled further and higher.'

Monsieur Etienne folds his arms. 'Are we that desperate in our research that we're now relying on your word? What on earth can a child – especially one like *you* – know about the mechanics of flight?'

'I don't know anything, monsieur,' I mutter, feeling my face go hot. 'Only what happened to me.'

'That's the point, Etienne,' Monsieur Joseph says. 'At this moment in time, neither do we. What we've been doing isn't working. I'm not convinced it ever will.'

'How do we know we can trust the girl?' Monsieur Etienne asks. 'She could be anyone.'

I feel his eyes on me again. Like they're peeling back the layers and finding a rotten little thief at the core. I don't like it. Maybe this place isn't right for me after all. Maybe I should go and face my old life again.

But as I turn to leave, Monsieur Etienne's quicker.

'Oh no you don't.' He blocks my exit. 'You think you're going to run off and take our secrets with you?'

'I wouldn't do that!' I cry.

'Course she wouldn't! Pierre agrees.

'I think we can trust the girl,' Monsieur Joseph says. 'Her quick action saved Pierre's life, after all.'

I'm touched by their loyalty, I really am. It makes me want to prove them right, that I *am* on their side. And that's a new sensation too.

Monsieur Etienne, I can tell, isn't sure about me at all. But there's a buzz in the room now. Where it's come from – my account or Monsieur Etienne's confidence – I don't know. I just hope there'll be no more talk of giving up.

'We'd better get a move on,' Monsieur Etienne says, as if confirming it. 'Otherwise the English will beat us to it, and then we'll be the *second* inventors of a flying contraption. No one will even remember our names.'

THREE

FOR A LETTER

6

As I start work that morning, the Montgolfiers are still hesitating over theirs. Pierre brings me regular updates throughout the day.

'They're arguing,' he tells me. 'Papa wants to think things over and not rush, Uncle Etienne's insisting they get a move on.'

I nod because I'm trying to listen *and* concentrate on the tasks I've been given to do. Behind the house is a cobbled yard, and beyond it an orchard, full of olive and cherry trees. It's here the Montgolfiers keep animals meant for the table, and I'm now the one responsible for feeding them. There are chickens and a goose, and a couple of goats kept for their milk. My favourite is the sweet-faced lamb who likes to nibble people's toes.

'I've called her Lancelot,' I tell Pierre.

He pulls a face. '*Lancelot?* For a girl?'

'Yes, *for a girl.*'

'But in the story Lancelot is a man – a brave knight.'

I don't know what story he's on about; I'm thinking of the pâtisserie with the chestnut cakes, the ones I'd promised myself once Madame Delacroix had paid me. But I don't press the point. My arm's still weak, so having Pierre here is a help for the carrying-buckets part of things. What's not so good is Voltaire, who I swear is trying to make Coco jealous by sticking close to my ankles. It makes my rooster nervous. Inside his sling I feel his claws twitching, which is a sure sign trouble's brewing.

It's Odette who shows me my next job. Thursdays are extra busy, she tells me. Not only is there the usual five-course luncheon to prepare, but it's also wash day. And Madame Verte runs a very tight household. The housekeeper is small with a sharp chin and sunken mouth that makes her look like she's just sipped vinegar. She's possibly the only person in the world Odette is scared of.

'You'd better get rid of that chicken of yours,' Odette warns me under her breath. 'The only animals Madame Verte allows in the kitchen are dead ones for the pot.'

'Oh, let him stay. He's no trouble,' I plead.

Yet, sure enough, the moment Madame Verte spots Coco she asks: 'Why isn't that bird plucked yet? It should've been in the oven an hour ago.'

Which makes me realize the kitchen's really not safe for Coco. Back outside he goes. I take him as far as the orchard.

'Sorry boy,' I tell him. 'I'll save you some decent scraps.'

Without so much as a backwards glance, he struts over to Lancelot. The lamb sniffs his feet, and he quite happily lets her, then settles between her front hooves like she's the comfiest, cosiest cushion in the world. The rate he falls asleep there is astonishing – far quicker than he nods off in *my* arms. I try not to be offended.

What Odette hasn't mentioned about laundry is how much the hot water and lye stings your hands. Nor does she tell me the wash is almost entirely made up of Madame Montgolfier's undergarments. For both these reasons I get it done as quick as I can.

Odette then informs me it's started to rain.

'Hang everything up there.' She points to a drying rack suspended from the ceiling. It's close enough to the fire to catch the heat from it, so with arms full of dripping chemises and petticoats and nightgowns, I climb onto a stool to hang the laundry. It's funny to think I've not even clapped eyes on Pierre's mother, yet here I am handling her most private things.

I've just finished when Monsieur Joseph comes into the kitchen, carrying a notebook.

'I hate to complain, Madame Verte,' he says, putting the notebook on the table and holding up his hands in defeat. 'But the porridge at breakfast was a little too hot.' Monsieur Joseph eats all his meals cold – it's a household fact, so Pierre told me. Apparently warm food gives his father wind.

Madame Verte listens, stony faced. When he's gone, she takes her irritation out on me.

'Who on earth put those wet things up there?' She's spotted the undergarments, which to my novice eye are drying nicely.

'It's raining, Madame,' I say.

'We still peg it out, it never rains for long.' Madame Verte sighs crossly. 'Leave it for now. There are dishes that need doing. And next time ask Odette if you're not sure.'

As I'm cussing Odette for her bad advice, I notice Monsieur Joseph has left his notebook behind. It's on the kitchen table, temptingly within reach. Perhaps his argument with Monsieur Etienne cleared the air and he *has* got down to work. Maybe the design for a brand new prototype is here inside this very book!

Once I'm sure Madame Verte isn't watching, I sneak a quick look. My eyes shoot straight to the pictures. They're done by the same hand as the others I saw that day in the lane. And just like them they leap from the paper like magic. I flick through page after page of flying creations – oblongs, spheres, one like a teardrop, which seems to be the favourite because Monsieur Joseph's sketched it a lot. There are plenty of angry crossings out too.

I keep turning the pages.

Then, suddenly, that's it. The rest of the book is blank. The very last entry is of an oblong shape with ropes in each corner. Recognizing it, my chest tightens. At the end of the ropes dangle a boy and a girl.

Pierre. And me.

There are no notes with the drawing, just one single word that looks like this: *Fini*.

I don't know what it means. But I'm sad. All that excitement and wonder, and then – nothing. A dead end. When Madame Delacroix saw the papers that night she thought the Montgolfiers had been busy – she said as much. But that's just it – they haven't. There must be something we can do to get them working again.

'How's that laundry coming on? First lot dry yet?' Odette calls from the other side of the kitchen.

'What? Oh.' I glance up at the ceiling rack. 'Almost. Just a bit . . .'

I go silent.

Something bizarre has happened to Madame M's undergarments. They're full like a ship's sail in a storm. And growing bigger right before my eyes! Twitching, wafting – a little upwards, a little sideways – it's as if they've got a life of their own.

Any minute Madame Verte'll notice and tell me *that's* why I should've hung the washing outside. But I can't stop staring. What's happening is just like the flying contraption in miniature. The garments lift then sink. But there's a difference. Madame M's silk chemise is bulging like a sausage skin. Yet the cotton petticoat hanging next to it has hardly moved. Why is this happening? I don't know much about laundry, but I'm sure it isn't meant to move by itself.

Grabbing a pencil from the pot on the table, I open the notebook on its next clean page. I draw the stove. The pots. The pans. Then the laundry rack above it. Squinting, I try to guess distances, heights.

'Magpie!' Madame Verte barks. 'What are you up to?'

I start. The notebook slips from my hand to the floor. Ducking down to grab it, I'm too late. A wooden clog rests on top of it.

'What's this?' says Odette.

I lunge at her feet. 'Don't!'

Too quick for me, she snatches the book away. 'Not drawing undergarments, are you?'

I make a grab for the book again.

She grins. 'You *were*, weren't you? Oh, I reckon this is worth sharing.'

I don't even get the chance to turn pink. There's a whoosh of air right next to my head and Madame Verte boxes my ears so hard my cap goes flying across the room.

'This is a kitchen, not an art *salon!*' Madame Verte cries.

I know I should be acting sorry, but instead I'm watching Odette. She's staring at the drying rack, her mouth a funny 'O' shape. I follow her gaze. The chemise is now so full it's lifted off the rack entirely and floats up, before coming to rest against the ceiling.

'*Mon Dieu!*' I'm on tiptoes, amazed. What if there was no ceiling? What if that chemise kept rising up and up into the sky?

Odette though, begins to scream. 'It's a ghost! Oh my goodness, a ghost!'

She goes on and on, until Madame Verte sloshes brandy into a glass and tells her to drink it in one gulp. Meanwhile, I'm told to stand on the dresser and poke at the chemise with a broom, until it falls in a grimy heap to the floor. Once she realizes the kitchen isn't haunted, Odette soon recovers.

'You're a stupid little creature,' she spits at me. 'You can't even do the laundry properly.'

I'm rapidly going off her, however hard she works.

'At least I'm not scared of a chemise,' I point out.

Odette pinches me hard on the leg.

'Stop it, the pair of you!' Madame Verte yells.

The kitchen door opens. Hovering at the top of the steps is Monsieur Etienne, pocket watch in his hand. Madame Verte's back visibly stiffens.

'Lunch is rather late today.' He gestures to the time. 'We're quite famished, *dear* Madame Verte.'

'We had a few teething problems this morning, Monsieur,' Madame Verte explains in a simpering voice I've not heard her use before.

I'm just thankful the chemise is now soaking in a bucket. Odette, though, can't keep her gob shut. 'Magpie's been drawing things.'

My fist closes around the notebook in my pocket, wishing it was her face.

'Drawing eh?' Monsieur Etienne comes on down the steps.

'Umm . . . not exactly.' I want to say how the silk had floated upwards when the cotton hadn't. That the heat of the fire had done something to make it rise. But I don't know how to explain it. It's easier just to take out the notebook and show him my sketches, which I do.

'Do you see how the garments rose up?' I rush through each drawing, I'm that nervous. 'It's because the air's hot. It must be!'

'I'll have my brother's notebook back, *merci*,' he says when I'm done, and lifts it, and all my findings, from my hands. 'And Madame Verte? Luncheon, please, as quick as you can!' Then he turns heel and leaves.

I stare after him, frustrated. I'm not convinced he was even listening to me.

Yet on the way back up the stairs when he thinks no one's looking, he stops and opens the notebook. *I'm* watching. He's staring at my pictures. Head tilted, finger tapping the page, he drinks them in. When he's finished, he looks up, catches my eye and nods. My face warms: I think maybe it's his way of saying well done.

7

One morning, a week or so later, Pierre catches me whistling as I sweep the yard.

'What're you cheery about?' He takes the broom from me, and gestures for me to sit with him on the wall.

'I can't. Madame Verte'll have my guts for garters,' I tell him, very firmly taking the broom back again.

He pulls a hurt face. 'Work more important than your friends now, eh?'

'It's not like that,' I try to explain. 'Work *and* friends – they're both important, it's not a contest. I don't want to cause trouble. I like it here. Really like it.'

I could also tell him that, for once, I feel part of something decent and good. All right, so my hands are all blisters and my back aches, but if this is what

66

honest work feels like then I like it. At least you're not forever looking over your shoulder. Best of all, we're *this* close to what could be one of the greatest inventions on earth – if the Montgolfiers get on with it, that is. But I see Pierre's understood because he's smiling now.

'I'll leave you to it,' he says. Calling Voltaire, the two of them stroll off to read poetry or whatever it is they do in the mornings. Out of habit, I scan the yard for Coco. He'd been happily pecking the dust before Pierre and Voltaire arrived. Now he's nowhere to be seen.

The orchard's the obvious spot, he's too lazy to go further. And let's not forget Lancelot's there, who he's taken a real shine to, but I find her all alone under the olive trees.

'Where's he gone?' I ask her. She nuzzles my toes, briefly, politely, then goes back to grazing with little dainty bites. It's like watching a lady eat cake.

I walk on through the trees to the bottom of the orchard. I'm starting to get annoyed now. I've got work to do. If Coco can't be trusted then he'll have to stay in the sling.

'Thought I'd forgotten you, eh?'

Madame Delacroix's voice makes me freeze mid-step. I spin round. Can't see where it's coming from. As she clears her throat, I catch sight of her, back against the orchard wall. She's got Coco by his heels. She's holding him upside down so his wings splay out.

'Put him down,' I say, low and furious.

I step slowly towards her. I'm fighting the urge to rush and grab him, and scratch her eyes out for good measure. Despite the heat of the day she's got gloves on again. The leather is dark purplish, like raw liver. She doesn't move. She's in charge and knows it. It's a clever hiding spot she's chosen because you can't see it from the house.

Once I'm within snatching distance I hold out my arms. 'Please, give him to me.'

'We have a deal, don't we?' Madame Delacroix says, ignoring my plea. 'Has it slipped your mind?'

I don't answer. I'd tried my best to forget about it, yes, but it's flooding back now like toothache you'd thought had gone.

'What d'you want from me? Can't you just leave me alone?' I ask, bitterly.

'I hired you to do a job and that job isn't finished. You still work for me.'

'Not any more I don't.'

'Now, now, no need to be unfriendly,' she replies. 'You agreed to fetch a red leather box. You failed the first time, so you'll try again.'

I shake my head. 'I won't do it.'

'You know how some things are important to us, Magpie?' She says it gently. Yet the squeeze she gives Coco's feet makes him flinch in pain.

'Stop it!' I cry.

'I need that box,' she says.

I can't bear to see Coco upside down any longer. But I won't go against the Montgolfiers, either. I can't thieve from the very people who've given me this chance of a life where, for once, I'm *not* a criminal.

'I can't work for you,' I say again. My voice is shaking. 'I'm working here now. Anyway, you never did pay me.'

She tightens her grip on Coco once more. Though I beg her to stop, she keeps squeezing. I can't stand it. Just when I'm about to punch her, she says, 'How about I go inside and tell your new master what you really are, eh? What you took from here that night?'

My clenched fist falls to my side. She knows she's hit home.

'You don't want that, do you? But because I'm feeling generous, Magpie, I'll give you a few more days.'

The back door slams. Someone's coming: I glance behind to see who. Madame Delacroix lets go of Coco, who falls fluttering at my feet. By the time I've scooped him up, kissed and soothed him, she's gone.

Madame Verte is at the orchard gate, holding a

couple of empty pails. '*Vite,* Magpie! I need you! More water please!'

'Coming, Madame Verte.' I'm glad to be summoned.

The rest of the morning I'm flat-out busy collecting fruit, water, firewood, but I can't stop thinking about Madame Delacroix's demand. The thief in me knows I *could* get the box for her. It wouldn't be as hard as last time now I'm actually living in the house. I could pretend to be on an errand or wait till night-time again. I'm not even bothered about the payment. I just want her to leave Coco and me alone.

But.

I can't repay the Montgolfiers like this. Just thinking about it gives me the guilts so bad I feel sick. It's awful enough knowing I've stolen from them before. I couldn't live with myself if I did it again.

Why does she want the blasted box, anyway? What *wrong* have the Montgolfiers done her that's so set her on revenge?

The thing I do know is this: she only mentioned going back for the box once she'd seen the drawings. Which makes me think this is all about the invention. It's too much of a coincidence to be anything else, though the papers I'd snatched in panic weren't the right ones.

70

No, the drawings *she* wants are still in the box. Perhaps she's a spy like Pierre was talking about: if so, then this decides it for me, fair and square. There's no way I'll steal information so she can sell it to the English. I might be a thief but I'm not about to become a traitor to France.

By the time the town clocks strike two, the sky is a hard, hot blue. I'm exhausted.

'Rest time, Magpie!' Madame Verte calls from the back step.

Inside, the other servants are sat around the kitchen table eating, but it's too clattery and noisy, like the inside of my head. What I need is quiet.

Taking my bread and cheese back out to the orchard, I sit cross-legged under the fruit trees. Coco and Lancelot keep me company as I dream up ways of avoiding Madame Delacroix.

'What would you do, eh?' I ask the sheep as I feed her my bread crusts. She looks like she's chewing it over, before nuzzling my foot, so gentle and kind, my eyes fill up. If only people were as thoughtful as sheep.

We've just finished eating when Pierre appears. He flops down dramatically like he's got something important to say. Voltaire does the same, which makes Coco dart underneath Lancelot's fleece to hide.

From his jacket pocket, Pierre pulls out a news-sheet

and spreads it over the grass. 'Today's news, Magpie,' he sounds stressed, 'is of a most awful kind.'

I don't like his tone.

'We've got serious competition,' he says grimly. 'The English have already built a true-to-scale model of their flying machine. Reports from across the Channel say they're now within days of a practice flight. *Days!*'

Horrified, I glance down at the news-sheet. He's right, this is awful news, though to my eyes it's all just a jumble of ink on the page, until Pierre gestures to the big words in bold. 'Our only hope is this bit.'

'What bit?'

'It says the current model keeps losing air. They can't get it to stay aloft for longer than a few minutes – yet. But that's the point – they're working on it. And we're not.'

My heart sinks, then bobs right up again when I remember Monsieur Etienne's face on the stairs. 'Has your uncle told you about the laundry?'

Pierre looks puzzled. '*Laundry?*'

All right, so he hasn't. I'm irked. Shouldn't Monsieur Etienne be exploring last week's discovery? Seeing where it leads?

So, I tell Pierre the whole story. Even when I've finished, he still looks confused. 'You've been studying my mother's undergarments?'

'She has a lot of them,' I remark.

'That's because she rarely gets out of bed to wear anything else.'

I'd guessed as much, having seen the trays go up and down stairs at meal times. No one has ever said what's wrong with her, though.

'Is she dying?' I ask.

'*Zut alors*, Magpie!' Pierre yelps. 'Must you be so direct?'

'Sorry.' I flush, embarassed.

He's quiet for a moment, fidgeting with a stalk of grass. 'Her babies come too soon, that's the problem. It's why I've got no brothers or sisters.'

'I'm sorry,' I say again because it's awful sad. No wonder Monsieur Joseph was so shaken by Pierre falling from the rope that day. It must've given him the shock of his life.

'Anyway,' Pierre says more brightly. 'Tell me about the laundry again – and do it slowly this time.'

I'm about to start when the sound of hoof beats distracts us both. Coming down the driveway is a cloud of dust with legs – four of them, to be exact. It's a person on horseback. Both eager to see who it is, we go to the orchard gate.

The horse clatters into the yard, sending chickens flapping in all directions. Jumping down, the rider leads his horse to the water trough. They look like they've come a long way – the horse is sweaty and drinks deeply. The man is brown with dust.

'Take this letter to your master, will you?' he says, holding out a surprisingly clean, white letter. 'It's from Versailles. News has reached the King of the Mont-golfiers' flying creation. He is intrigued to know more by reply of post.'

I eye him suspiciously. The man's far too grubby to have come from the King. As if we'd hand over information just like that! How do we know he's not thick with the English?

'The King?' I fold my arms. I'm getting wise to this business now. 'What, as in King Louis of France?'

The messenger gives me a long, snooty look. 'Is there someone here with a brain I can speak to?'

'I'll take the message,' Pierre pipes up.

'No you won't!' I hiss under my breath. 'We don't know who he is yet.'

'For the love of all that's sacred!' the man cries, waving the letter at us. 'I'm Viscount Herges, assistant to the King!'

'You expect us to believe—'

Pierre cuts in. 'What an honour to receive news from Versailles, *merci*.' And he takes the offered letter, which I see now is sealed with the royal symbol – the one that's on real coins and badly faked ones.

I feel the blood drain from my face. This man really

is the King's messenger. I'm totally agog. I would've stayed staring in amazement, too, but luckily Pierre seizes my arm.

'We'll take the message to my father at once,' Pierre says. 'He's working very hard. We can hardly tear him away from his study to eat!'

This isn't true, and we both know it. Monsieur Joseph shuffles about the house each day looking more worried than ever. And Monsieur Etienne, enthusiastic though he is, doesn't seem to have actually *done* anything. Everything's just as it was: stuck.

Leaving Viscount Herges with his horse, we hurry inside. Safe in the kitchen, Pierre stops to turn the letter anxiously in his hand. 'I can't give this to Papa, Magpie.'

Now I'm the one who's puzzled. Surely a personal letter from the King is a *good* thing? One look at Pierre and I see it's not.

'You heard what was in today's news-sheet,' he wails. 'The English are just days away from beating us. They'll be the ones with their names in the history books. Can you imagine how terrible that will be for France?'

I admit it does sound bad.

'It's obviously why the King's got involved,' Pierre says, sounding more gloomy by the second. 'He's putting the pressure on us.'

'That might be a good thing, though?' I dare to suggest.

Pierre shakes his head. 'It'll panic Papa, that's all it'll do. He'll shrink into himself and then we'll make even less progress.'

I'm not sure that's possible.

'What about Monsieur Etienne?' I ask. 'Can't he do some work on the hot air idea? He's got my sketches to follow.'

Pierre rolls his eyes. 'Uncle Etienne's a business-man, Magpie. He knows the price of everything, who to speak to, how to sell an idea. But he knows next to nothing about science. That's probably why he didn't tell me about the undergarments. He won't have understood it well enough to explain it.'

'Oh!' I'm completely taken aback and, I don't mind admitting, almost a bit pleased. So much for girls like me knowing nothing. But it doesn't help us. Poor Pierre looks frustrated enough to cry.

'If we let King Louis down. If we don't make France proud, well . . .' he trails off.

'Well, what?'

'The King has prisons for people who displease him. There's talk too of a new execution device that cuts off heads in one swoop.'

It sounds a bit far-fetched to me, but I can see how upset Pierre is.

'Tell you what. You do the writing, I'll think up the words,' I say, rolling up my sleeves.

He looks horrified. '*We* answer the letter, d'you mean? Surely that's forgery.'

I give him my best hard stare.

'But Magpie, we can't—'

I interrupt. 'That Viscount person's outside waiting for a reply.'

So, taking a deep breath, Pierre cracks open the wax seal. Unfolded, the paper smells of leather and horse sweat. Just seeing the King's writing looping across the page is enough to amaze me. The message is short. I insist Pierre read it out loud.

Monsieurs Montgolfier,

My sources tell me our English neighbours across the Channel are on the cusp of a great aeronautical discovery. I am certain you share my concern that this is not good news for France. All we can hope is that they do not solve the issue of maintaining air inside the bag. I trust you will join me in praying for such an outcome.

Meanwhile, I have it on good authority that you are advancing with your own invention. It is in the very best interests of our nation that your work should be soon completed in preparation for a test flight here at Versailles.

The first bit we as good as know from the news-sheet.

The last part though sends us both into a spin.

'Versailles?' I gasp. '*Alors!*'

Pierre's gone such a pasty colour I'm worried he's about to faint.

'Right,' I say, because sounding purposeful helps. 'Let's get started.'

Searching the kitchen table drawers, Pierre can't find a pen or ink.

'Use pencil.' I give him one from Madame Verte's pot. 'And keep it brief – your papa's too busy to write at length, remember.'

'All right, Mademoiselle Bright Ideas, what shall we say?'

I think for a moment. '*Dear King* . . . no . . . *Your Majesty* is better . . . *Air issue almost remedied. You shall be the very first to know of our* . . .' I pause. 'What's a fancy word for very soon?'

'Imminent.'

'. . . *of our imminent success. Expect to hear from us within days.*'

The letter done, Pierre folds it neatly and takes it back outside.

'What do we do now?' Pierre asks as we watch Viscount Herges disappear off down the driveway.

'That stonking great lie we just told?' I reply confidently, 'We make sure it comes true.'

8

Yet before we get chance to start work, Monsieur Joseph makes a surprise announcement: he *is* building a brand-new prototype, after all.

'He's determined to find a way to fill the structure with warm air.' Pierre brings me the news in the kitchen garden where I'm cutting salad for lunch. 'It's the heat part of things he's interested in.'

'I wonder where he got *that* idea from,' I remark, though I'm thrilled something's happening at last.

A couple of afternoons later, Monsieur Joseph holds a test flight outside. All of us household staff gather in the yard because we're not going to miss this for the world. The prototype is a rectangle shape, made of paper moulded onto a wooden frame. The plan, so Monsieur Joseph announces, is to create smoke from

79

a fire. The smoke, being warm air, should cause the prototype to lift.

Should.

I'm expecting a bonfire, but what Monsieur Joseph attaches with ropes to the base of the paper shape is a shallow metal tray about the size of a cartwheel. On it, Monsieur Etienne places red-hot coals from the kitchen range. The whole thing looks wobbly, clumsy. Yet amazingly, on the count of three when the Montgolfiers release it, the prototype rises.

At least it does until Madame Verte says, 'What's that burning smell?'

'*Sacré bleu*!' Monsieur Joseph cries. 'It's catching fire!'

All that paper. All that wood. It burns quicker than a pork chop in a pan.

Once all the fuss and bad tempers die down, we're back to where we started: the Montgolfiers have no more new ideas, so it's up to Pierre and me to think of one: the King is waiting for news.

'We need wood and string,' I tell Pierre, as we start planning that same afternoon, 'and as much paper as you can manage.'

For this he sets off to the Montgolfier's mill, where apparently there's paper in piles as high as the ceiling. We're going to remake the original flying object, the one that caused the accident that day. Only ours will be much smaller so it'll be quick to put together and easy to hide. We'll also try to solve the hot air problem. Since Pierre's refused to let his feet leave the ground ever again, it's my job to size up trees in the orchard. I'm looking for one that's an easy climb with a decent height on it.

'What d'you think, Coco?' I ask, stopping by an olive tree. 'Will this do us?'

Coco's answer is to stroll over to Lancelot, who's keeping cool in the shade of a cherry tree. It's a reasonable sized one with low branches at the base. It's the perfect tree for our experiment; I like to think the animals helped us choose it.

It's not long before Pierre returns with what we need. With the rest of the household now having their overdue afternoon kip, the house is still, the blinds down at the windows. We've probably got a clear hour to ourselves.

Joining Lancelot and Coco under the cherry tree, we get to work. The first attempts don't go well. The paper keeps tearing. The wood won't flex. What we end up with is a shape that looks like a hat box that someone's stamped on.

Pierre sits back on his heels, frowning. 'There's no way on earth that's going to fly.'

'It doesn't matter if it's not perfect,' I say, trying to

keep his spirits up.

'But we promised the King,' Pierre groans. 'We said we'd have—'

'*Imminent news*,' I interrupt. 'Yes – and so we will if we keep trying.'

At moments like these he's just like Monsieur Joseph. He can't see past the worry. Voltaire, I notice, has given up watching us and waddled off. The other two animals are sound asleep.

'Right,' I get to my feet, brushing dust from my skirts. 'Pass me that paper – the big sheet of the thick stuff. Come on, look lively!'

And so, together, we try again.

This time we make an egg-shaped structure. I've seen shapes like it in the front few pages of Monsieur Joseph's notebook so it's got to be worth a try. Certainly, it's a lot easier to make. It doesn't look like it'll fall to pieces, either.

'Let's try it with the hot water,' I say.

'Is the structure strong enough?' Pierre asks.

'Won't know until we try.' This I call back over my shoulder. I'm already on my way to the kitchen for what we need next. I'm after a dish with handles; the one for serving meat in is perfect. The kettle on the stove is hot, so I take that too.

Back in the orchard, we tie rope to the wooden

frame of the structure, then I climb the cherry tree. It's not easy with the bulky egg-shape under arm, and I scratch my shins to shreds on the branches. But I'm too excited to care. While I'm still just within reach, Pierre hands me up the dish full of hot water. Securing the ends of rope round the handles, the bowl now hangs beneath the structure. Voltaire seems to have reappeared in time to watch disapprovingly.

Yet we know paper floats. It's light and strong, but doesn't stay airborne for long. Warm air seems to make things rise – Madame M's undergarments were proof of it. Using the two things together just might do the trick.

'Get ready to start counting, Pierre.' I take a deep breath. 'Five . . . four . . . three . . . two . . .'

I swing the prototype skywards. The dish tips madly. Water spills on the branches, on me. The whole thing, somehow, drags itself free of the tree, out into the open sky. Then it drops. I groan out loud. It's not working.

'Watch out!' I call to Pierre as it heads right for him.

He's grinning. 'No, *you* watch out, Magpie! It's coming your way!'

Before my eyes, the shape's beginning to lift again. It not the wind deciding where it goes: this time, it moves with purpose. It sails past me, past the tree itself. Soon it's twenty feet or so above us in the air.

I'm up there with it. Or at least my heart is, fluttering away like a skylark. I know what it's like to see rooftops, trees, rivers from above, animals so small they look like toys. I know that funny, lurching feeling and the strange, breathy quiet. It makes my toes tingle.

'*Zut alors*, look at it!' Pierre gasps.

'Don't speak!' I yell. 'Keep counting!'

Suddenly though, things don't look right. Our egg shape is at a queer angle. What should've been nicely puffed paper is collapsing in on itself.

'No!' I'm desperate for it to stay flying. 'Keep going!'

But the paper is covered in spreading dark patches. The steam, I realize, has made the paper wet. Our prototype isn't strong any more. One of the ropes tears away, leaving the dish hanging. The whole thing sinks steadily, swooping between the trees, bumping over the yard wall. I scramble down the tree just in time to hear *plop-crack* as it hits the cobbles.

'I counted two minutes and twelve seconds of flight!' Pierre cries.

'It's a start,' I admit. We've done all right, but I can't help but think it's not enough to impress the King.

Pierre though, grins from ear to ear. 'It flew, Voltaire!' he says, scooping up his duck and sitting him on his shoulder like some conquering hero. 'Our experiment worked!'

In the yard, we're greeted with a mess of broken china and splattered paper. Pierre prods it with his foot.

'Leave it. I'll tidy up,' I tell him, bustling him inside; I don't want him to see I'm disappointed. We need to do better next time. And that's the problem – there aren't many 'next times' before it's too late.

Our experiment *was* better than Monsieur Joseph's effort earlier, I tell myself as I start sweeping. The steam must be doing something right.

'MAGPIE!'

I go stiff. The shriek coming from behind me is Madame Verte's. She's heading my way, her footsteps the fast, furious kind that tell me I'm in trouble. I brace myself for a thick ear, so when she pushes two empty buckets into my hands instead, I'm startled.

'Water!' she cries. 'Quickly! Get heating as much as you can!'

I nod and take the buckets. I don't ask why. Then she's turned heel and rushed back inside and I just hope she didn't see what remains of the blue and white serving dish when, honest to God, she almost stepped in it.

Back in the kitchen, Odette's adding more wood to the stove. It's already blazing: the heat coming off it makes me sweat.

'We need that water upstairs for Madame M,'

Odette says, wiping her brow. 'Bring it up when it's hot, can you? Quick as you like!'

I realize with growing dread this isn't bathwater we're heating.

'Is she all right?' I ask.

Odette's eyes fill with tears. 'We've sent for the doctor – he's with her now.'

Despite the scorching stove, the water takes forever to warm. As I wait, toes tapping, I churn over what Pierre told me about his mama. Such a pity she can't have more babies. Poor Pierre, too. He'd make a smashing big brother. Which then gets me thinking about being a sister myself. Not that it'd ever happen, but I wouldn't half mind finding out.

On the stairs, I meet Odette, who takes the pails of water from me, giving me an armful of bloody sheets in return.

'Don't look so horrified,' she says, smiling. 'The doctor's just told us he thinks the baby will be fine.'

I'm so glad I start to well up myself.

Madame Verte then appears with orders from Monsieur Joseph for a celebratory lunch to be served tomorrow.

'Let me help, will you? I'd really like to,' I say.

'You're a good girl, Magpie,' Madame Verte pats me on the shoulder, then turns to Odette. 'When you've taken that water in, can you send word to Monsieur

Couteau? We need him here first thing tomorrow.'

Odette frowns. 'The butcher? I can wring a chicken's neck good as he can.'

'We're not having chicken,' Madame Verte announces. 'We're having lamb.'

It takes a moment to sink in. We've only got one lamb.

'You can't eat Lancelot!' I burst out.

'Lancelot?' Odette's eyebrows shoot up. 'Who's *that*?'

But I'm frantic. 'She's the prettiest sheep you'll ever see! And honestly, she's kind too and nibbles your feet! Coco adores her! Please, you can't do this!'

Odette snorts. Madame Verte folds her arms. 'What's all this silliness?'

'She's named the sheep *Lancelot*!' Odette laughs.

They look at me like I'm madder than the King of England.

9

From that moment on I'm downright miserable. It's daft, I know, because I've never *ever* turned my nose up at a lamb chop. And with a baby Montgolfier on the way now, there's lots to be glad about. Yet the next morning, seeing Lancelot in the orchard like she doesn't know what's coming, makes it ten times worse. As usual, she bounds over and starts nosing my pockets for scraps. Then she butts Coco who's still asleep in his sling. She doesn't stop until he finally pokes his head out.

'You'd better say your goodbyes,' I tell her, scratching the spot she likes between the ears.

Reaching up, she nuzzles Coco's head oh so gently I can hardly bear to watch. Perhaps they *do* know what's coming, after all.

Thinking it's best to get on with it, I give Lancelot a quick brush down, check her feet, her teeth. Under Madame Verte's instructions I take her to the yard to weigh her. She comes in at just under twenty-eight pounds – Madame Verte was hoping she'd be thirty, at least – yet she's a fine healthy specimen with a good solid rump and strong flanks. And even now I can't help noticing her sweet nature, the sort you'd expect from a loyal pet dog. It's this that makes it so hard.

Just as I'm slipping a rope over her head, the front gate clanks shut. Normally it's a job to hear it from the orchard, but I'm on high alert: Monsieur Couteau's due any time. Sick with dread, I go to the orchard gate to check, just as a horse and rider pull up at the back door. Unless the butcher rides expensive look-ing steeds and dresses like Viscount Herges, then this visitor definitely isn't him.

Then comes the shout, 'Urgent message from the King!' And my panic turns into a different sort. I race into the yard, leaving Lancelot right where she is.

'I'll take it!' I offer, trying all the world this time to convince him I *do* have a brain. Thankfully he doesn't seem to remember me.

But before Viscount Herges can give me the note, the back door opens. Pierre, his father and his uncle stumble out into the morning, looking like they've already done a big fat slice of celebrating and not yet been to bed.

Frantic, I pull faces at Pierre. We can't let his father or uncle read that note. If they do, then they'll know what we've been up to, and we're not ready for that yet.

It's too late.

Monsieur Etienne has the letter in his hand. He cracks open the wax seal, shakes out the folded paper, draws himself up to his full, enormous height. At his elbow, Monsieur Joseph manages a weak smile.

'A message from King Louis, eh? This is an unexpected honour,' he says, though doesn't sound convinced.

Finally, Pierre catches on. His face drops. He looks to me. All I can do is shrug, helpless. We're about to be rumbled.

Clearing his throat Monsieur Etienne reads, '"*Monsieurs Montgolfier, Since our last correspondence events have taken a sorry turn here at Versailles . . ."*' Monsieur Etienne stops, confused. 'Last correspondence? Have you written on our behalf and not told me, brother?'

I keep my eyes glued to the ground.

'Why would I write to the King?' Monsieur Joseph asks. 'Good grief, I've been wanting to call a halt to our work, not draw attention to it!'

' "*. . . News that your invention for flight is progressing*

with a speed to rival the English is very pleasing to hear",
Monsieur Etienne reads on. In the silence that follows,
I risk glancing at Monsieur Joseph who looks like
someone's just walloped him across the back of the
head with a frying pan. Monsieur Etienne holds the
letter at arm's length, scowling. It's Pierre who speaks
first.

'We wrote to him,' he says meekly. 'Magpie and I. A
message came a few days ago wanting news of our
invention and we replied to it.'

I wince.

'You did *what*?' Monsieur Joseph gasps. 'Why? How?'

'It was my idea,' I speak up, not wanting Pierre to
take the blame. 'We told the King we were making
progress. And now we've done a test, see, with hot
water and it makes the flying last longer.'

'Progress?' Monsieur Joseph almost laughs. Then he
remembers Viscount Herges, who's still here, looking
alarmed, and calls Odette to take him inside for
refreshments. I dread to think what the Viscount
makes of us, or what he'll tell the King.

When he's safely out of earshot, Monsieur Joseph
lets rip. 'This is absurd! The prototype's not ready!
How DARE you tell the King of France it is!'

'But we thought . . .' I hesitate. What *did* we think?
That our experiment with a bit of paper and a serving
dish would save the day?

A wave of despair hits me. Thieving from these good people was wrong enough. This, though – lying to the king – well and truly takes the cake. We're completely out of our depth.

'There's more in the letter,' Monsieur Etienne tells us. I don't want to hear it. Nor does Pierre, who lets out a groan. '*"We are counting on you not simply to make the whole of France proud, but to also raise the spirits of a heartbroken Queen. My wife has sunk into a depression over the loss of her favourite pet. Her only remaining interest is in your flying machine, which I believe will be the best and only solution to her grief. I have, therefore, promised to host a demonstration here, at our Palace, in a week's time . . ."*'

One week?

This is getting worse by the second.

'Impossible!' Monsieur Joseph cries. 'We could hardly make the journey to Paris in that time – and that's if we actually had a prototype to take with us.'

'Which we don't,' Pierre mutters.

What an absolute dog's breakfast we've made of things. Now we're in this right up to our necks, which makes me think of prisons and those chopping machines again. I feel ill.

'We could ask for more time,' Monsieur Etienne suggests. 'Another few weeks?'

Bizarrely, he doesn't seem ruffled by the message. In fact he's looking. . . well . . . *excitable*. I wonder if he's still drunk from celebrating.

'Don't you see? This interest from the King could be our golden opportunity!' Monsieur Etienne's face lights up. 'Think of the crowds at Versailles! The important guests! The news reporters! It'll be all round the world in no time!'

I'm not sure what to make of this sudden heart-change.

Monsieur Joseph is less than convinced. 'The prototype's not safe—'

'So we make it safe!' Monsieur Etienne replies. 'Anyway, there won't be another accident because no one's asking us to send *people* up in the air. The English aren't that far ahead of us. It's the prototype that needs to fly, that's all!'

'Are you mad? How can we make a prototype in a week?' Monsieur Joseph cries.

'We'll help,' I say. 'Won't we, Pierre?' He nods eagerly, but Monsieur Joseph doesn't so much as glance our way.

'Just think Joseph, we'll be the ones who invented the first flying machine – us, not the English. And,' Monsieur Etienne raises a finger dramatically, 'Think of your unborn child. If his father is a national hero, then his future will be blessed.'

His? I think. What if the baby's a girl? What will *her* future be? Whatever happens though, Monsieur

93

Etienne's speech seems to have worked.

'All right, but we can't be rushed,' Monsieur Joseph mutters. 'We'll need to ask for more time. Nor can we be dictated to by Marie Antoinette's whims.'

'It's not a crime to be upset over an animal,' I point out

Pierre agrees: 'I'd be heartbroken if anything happened to Voltaire.'

We discuss what message to send. There's no denying the excitement that's suddenly buzzing between us as we all start to talk at once.

Then I see a lone man walking down the drive towards us. The sun glints off the knives strapped across his chest: this must be Monsieur Couteau. The grin on my face freezes right there.

'Magpie? You all right?' Pierre asks.

Under his arm is Voltaire: this gives me a sudden, desperate idea.

'Send the Queen a new pet.' I say before I've thought it through. 'That's what we should do. As a gift, I mean.'

Monsieur Etienne raises his eyebrows. 'A *pet*?'

'If we send her an animal to replace the one that died, she might feel happier to wait for us.'

Pierre – kind Pierre – sees my point: 'It might buy us a bit more time, Papa.'

Monsieur Joseph rubs his face wearily. 'What do you suggest we send, Magpie?'

I try not to look at Monsieur Etienne. Or at the butcher who's now reached us.

'Send Lancelot the lamb,' I reply. 'We can buy the chops in if we have to.'

Monsieur Joseph chews it over, slowly, painfully, till I can hardly bear it.

'We *must* send her, Papa!' Pierre agrees. 'She's a fine-looking beast – perfect for the Queen's model farm.'

Monsieur Joseph rolls his shoulders, glances at Monsieur Etienne who, amazingly, nods.

'It's an unusual way to do business,' he admits. 'But it's probably the best bargaining chip we've got.'

I almost sag with relief as Pierre and I beam at each other – big, fat, stupid-happy grins.

Convincing Viscount Herges is harder work: 'How on earth am I meant to carry a sheep all the way back to Paris?'

Yet before he can refuse entirely, we've organized a cart and wooden crate and Monsieur Couteau is sent away, his butcher's knives still sparkling clean. I give Lancelot a kiss on the muzzle, while Coco lands a peck on her ear. Voltaire keeps his distance from them both. I don't think he ever approved.

Feeling choked, I say to Lancelot, 'Be good. Be beautiful. Win the Queen's heart and make her happy again.'

Lancelot gazes up the driveway. She's not upset in the slightest, as far as I can tell. In fact – and I can't believe I've never noticed it before – with her chin in the air, she looks almost like royalty herself.

'You've sent our lamb to the Queen of France?' Madame Verte thinks it's a joke when I tell her. Her and Odette laugh so hard they have to dab their faces dry with their aprons. When she realizes I'm serious I'm told to go to the market for chops.

'Going to give them names too, are you?' Odette asks, which sets them both off again.

And, you know what, I don't mind. In fact, for once, I see the funny side.

10

The letter to the King changes everything. It's as if a pair of giant hands has seized the Montgolfiers and given them a very decent shake. The celebration lunch is postponed: instead, over the next few weeks, the house becomes a whirlwind of notetaking, shape-designing, dropping different-sized paper objects from the top of staircases in the hope that one at least will float on air.

We're all agreed now that hot air rises better than cold air. And that the heat needs to be the dry kind, though with this comes the risk of fire. What's needed is some way of keeping that hot air inside the prototype, which Monsieur Etienne has named 'le balloon'.

Each day, as I do my chores, Pierre seeks me out to

tell me the latest developments.

'It's more like a teardrop, only upside down,' Pierre explains one afternoon, drawing the shape with his toe in the dirt. 'But they're stuck on what to make it from – paper or cotton.'

I think of the laundry rack, full of undergarments. How the silk items floated up far better than the cotton ones. Paper, when we'd used it, didn't rise the same way, either.

I look at Pierre. 'Silk.'

'Pardon?'

'You need to make your object from stronger stuff than paper but not as strong or as heavy as cotton – silk. It's about the *strength* of the material,' I add, in case he hasn't got it.

Pierre stares at me, amazed. 'How do you know these things, Magpie?'

'I keep my eyes open, that's all.'

Though really it's living on the streets that's done it. You watch and listen. Look out for the things other people miss. Then, just when I don't want her to, Madame Delacroix looms in my head. The hairs lift on my arms like when the sun's gone in.

'Listen.' I drop my voice, scanning the gate, the hedges, the orchard just in case. 'Your pa and uncle are being careful, aren't they? With the drawings and the plans? They're not telling anyone?'

Pierre laughs. 'Of course they're being careful!'

'I hope so, because word gets around. Secrets get out.'

He sees I'm serious. 'What are you trying to tell me, Magpie?' And he looks right at me, then, like he knows something's wrong. I wonder – just for a moment – if I *could* tell him about Madame Delacroix. But I can't. Of course I can't. It'd mean admitting everything.

'We should do the opposite,' I blurt out. 'If we can't keep it secret, we should let everyone know. If everything's done in the open there'll be no secrets for the English to steal.'

Later that week, during a break in the balloon preparations, the celebration lunch is finally served. As it's a blazing summer's day, we've set up tables in the orchard that are groaning under all the food: tarts, cold meat, pastries, herb omelettes, salad from the garden, peaches, pistachio cake, and a platter of sizzling lamb chops.

Madame Verte, Odette and I are invited to stay and eat our meal at the far end of the table.

'Take that blasted chicken bag off for once,' Odette mutters to me. Reluctantly, I do as she says.

It *is* funny being here in the orchard with no Lancelot, but I don't feel sad. How can I, when

Monsieur Joseph is on his feet, glass of bubbly wine in hand, toasting his wife and baby.

'To my Maria,' he says, and turns back towards the house, to the far window that looks out over the town towards the river. A woman is sitting there.

'That's her,' Odette whispers as I crane my neck for a better look. 'Madame M.'

She's wearing a white chemise. Her hair is pretty – all dark and curling. Raising her hand, she gives us a little wave. I decide I like her: she looks the dead spit of Pierre.

Once the toast is over, I get up, thinking we need to tidy the food away. But Odette yanks me back into my seat again as, with a flip of the coat-tails, Monsieur Etienne stands.

'Dear friends,' he says in his silky-smooth way. 'On this auspicious day, I have one more piece of news to share.'

I glance at Pierre: he looks baffled.

'We could've done our first proper test flight here in the orchard. We could've aimed small. Instead, we've thrown ourselves into making the model at full size, which means we need a bigger space for flying it.'

He pauses like one of those street corner poets who stand on fish boxes, enjoying the sound their own voice makes.

'Today, I spoke to the Mayor. He's given us permission to demonstrate the prototype's first flight in Annonay's marketplace!'

There's a gasp around the table. Everyone cheers. Glasses are refilled and another toast made: 'To the marketplace!'

Yet my stomach starts doing odd fluttery things. It might be the lamb chops. Or that suddenly everything's got so big, so fast, because Annonay's marketplace is not for cowards. It's a big, hot, open space that on the quietest of days is still crawling with people.

Pierre cuts himself another slice of cake and shuffles round the table to sit with me.

'They've decided to make the prototype out of cotton *and* paper,' he says. 'Uncle Etienne thinks the silk'll be too costly for a practice run.'

'Oh.' I nod, though I don't know how the two fabrics will work together. They didn't do too well on their own.

Seeing I'm doubtful, Pierre gives me a nudge. 'I also told Uncle Etienne what you said about keeping secrets. That's why they've decided to make the test flight public.'

I force a smile. I know I should be pleased. And I am. Trouble is, it gets me thinking about other secrets, the ones I'm holding on to for dear life.

*

It's dark when we finally leave the table. I'm clearing the last of the dishes from the orchard when a figure steps out from behind a tree. I jump out of my wretched skin.

'Bravo, Magpie!' Madame Delacroix says, slow-clapping her gloved hands. It makes a thudding sound. 'What a charming celebration. Indeed, what a productive few weeks you've had! I've been watching it all.'

I edge away, making sure the table is between us.

'What're you doing here?' I croak, terrified some-one will see us.

Her gaze flicks towards the house. She doesn't come any closer. I think she might be nervous too.

'About that box you're collecting for me,' she says.

She knows I've not done it yet because I can't meet her eye. She licks her lips. Fixes me with her chips-of-ice-stare.

'I won't do it,' I say.

'I think you will,' she replies. 'After what I've seen here recently, I want that box more than ever.'

'I can't get it! It's imposs—'

Her hand flies out. She seizes me by the face, squeezing it hard like a lemon gone dry. Pain shoots through my skull. 'Don't test my patience, Magpie. I've given you more time and that time is up. Do as I say or I'll tell your dear Montgolfiers all about our little arrangement.'

'They won't believe you,' I manage to say.

'Course they will,' she sneers. 'Who'd listen to you, a brown-skinned little thief?'

I sob, panicked.

'I'll be watching you, Magpie. Mark my words.' She lets me go with a shove.

Then, back to being oh-so-respectable again, Madame Delacroix bids me a polite *bonne nuit*.

And that's the worst thing, it's as if *we're* the proper team, me and her, and with everyone else – Pierre, Madame Verte, even Odette – I'm just pretending. That's not how it is for me. Though caring about the people in this house, I'm beginning to see, brings a danger all of its own.

11

I don't sleep a wink that night. All the next morning I'm gritty and grouchy. Though I throw myself into my work, I still can't stop thinking about that blasted red box and why Madame Delacroix can't just clear off and leave me alone, though I'm pretty certain that's not going to happen. The closer we get to beating the English, the more desperate she'll become. The thought of it weighs me down.

A delivery from the mill brings roll after roll of paper, then, late morning, the fabric arrives. It's just the sort of distraction I'm after – yards of sackcloth-coarse cotton in gold, sky blue and brightest scarlet red, a sight that makes me grin with delight.

Yet the fabric's hard to work with: it takes four of us to hold a length straight, never mind all the cutting and threading to be done. We need helpers — and lots of them — which is where Monsieur Etienne's talents come in. Donning his smartest wig and brightest jacket, he heads off into Annonay to recruit helpers. In less than an hour he returns with a list of names as long as the river itself.

'They've all promised to be here by two o'clock,' he confirms.

Meanwhile, I'm taken from my normal duties and told to go to the haberdashers on Rue Montague to buy every single reel of thread. As Coco's been as moody and scratchy as me so far today, I don't suppose it'll hurt to leave him behind this once.

'Keep a close eye on him, won't you?' I ask Pierre. 'Put him in his sling if he looks worried.'

Pierre pulls a face. 'I'm not wearing that stinky old thing. Stop fussing, will you? You're going to the haberdashers, not Paris.'

The errand takes only half an hour. Yet by the time I get back, the yard's full of feathers: white ones, orange ones, and Pierre is crouched over a pail of water, bathing Voltaire's neck.

'What the heck's going on?' I cry, dropping my packages and rushing over.

There's lots of blood on Pierre's breeches and hands.

'They were out here, keeping away from each other. And then . . . BOOF! Coco went crazy at something. He turned on Voltaire,' Pierre clicks his fingers, 'Like that! Something must've scared him.'

I find Coco cowering under the hedge. He's got a bald spot on his wing, but thankfully it looks worse than it is.

'You daft bird,' I tell him. 'What spooked you, eh?' Though it doesn't take much guessing. Madame Delacroix, keeping her word, is watching everything.

'First, the paper and cotton must be sewn together. Then we'll sew each segment to create a teardrop structure,' Monsieur Etienne explains to our helpers when they arrive that afternoon. 'The stitching needs to be as neat and tight as it can be.'

There are too many people to fit in the salon, so they spread out around the house. It soon looks more like a workshop than a home. Everyone sits with their heads bent as if they're praying in church. It's as quiet as one too – you can almost hear the tug of needle through cloth and paper.

My job's to keep the workers refreshed with Madame Verte's pea broth served in little cups. As I need both hands for the tray, Coco stays in the kitchen in a box under the table. Madame Verte says she'll turn a blind eye for today, and I'm grateful because, after what happened earlier with Voltaire, the kitchen feels safer than the yard.

It's as I'm in the salon offering broth that a woman holds up her needle for me to see.

'This thread keeps breaking,' she says.

'Mine too,' someone else agrees.

'And mine,' chips in a woman sitting by the window. 'The stitches won't hold – look.'

Suddenly, everyone is criticizing the shoddy thread.

'But I bought it from the haberdashers in town,' I try to explain. 'Honestly, it's the proper stuff.'

'For darning petticoats maybe,' says the woman who'd complained first. 'This won't hold together no flying machine.'

The work stops. People sit back in their seats, lean against walls, arms folded in protest. I don't know what to say, or if they'd listen to me even if I did.

The first Montgolfier I find is Monsieur Joseph, who's in the room next door with Pierre, measuring lengths of rope. I tell him what's happened.

'That won't do at all.' Leaving the rope, he stuffs his hands deep into his pockets, suddenly thoughtful.

'We need stronger thread, papa. It's not a problem,' says Pierre.

'Where will we get that from?' he frets. 'We've already bought every reel the haberdasher had.' He turns to me. 'Was there no other thread in the shop, Magpie? No twine? No string? No ribbons?'

'*Ribbons?*' I can't help but frown. 'No, monsieur, just buttons.'

Looking down at his frock coat, he inspects his own buttons. They're gold. Shiny. One by one he does them up. In the same order, he undoes them again. I glance at Pierre, who shrugs: neither of us know what he's thinking.

'How many buttons did the haberdasher have?' Monsieur Joseph asks, still looking at his coat.

'I don't know; I didn't count them. Trays full, though.'

A smile lifts the corners of his mouth. 'Trays full, eh?'

'Trays full, monsieur, yes.'

I guess what's coming next.

It turns out each tray holds one thousand buttons – or thereabouts. To be certain we have enough I lug three trays up the hill. The helpers, back on side once they see the task will work, stay well into the night to sew. Row after row of tiny buttons are stitched on to each segment, then that segment is fastened to another and so on until the massive teardrop shape is complete.

'We've used eight hundred and twenty-seven reels of thread, and a whopping two thousand buttons,' I tell Pierre when everything's finished. 'What d'you make of that?'

He tries to grin but it turns into a yawn. 'Sometimes Magpie, I think you know too much.'

The morning of the demonstration dawns another fine, clear summer's day. A good omen, I'm hoping with every scrap of my being. I hardly slept last night, either. Excitement kept me awake this time. So did the nerves. If we don't fly this balloon today I'm likely to go off like a Catherine wheel.

We eat breakfast all together, which makes me feel that, for today at least, I'm not only the girl who feeds the animals; I'm part of something so huge it's going to make history. Just to think of it: by sundown the name 'Montgolfier' on every news-sheet, Madame Montgolfier's silk petticoats the talk of France. The English, beaten, will have no need of our secrets. Madame Delacroix will give up and crawl back under whichever stone she came from. It's thoughts like these that make me push my plate away. I can't eat a single crumb.

At six o'clock we go outside and start loading our equipment into carts. We don't see the carriage pulling up at the gate — not until a man starts shouting: 'I'm here on King Louis' orders to seize the Messieurs Montgolfier!'

Everyone stops in surprise. The carriage is a smart, black one. Another man in the King's livery jumps down from the driver's seat. I'm alarmed, but only for a moment, because at least this time we've got news that should satisfy the King: the prototype has been built, and the proof is right here to see.

Monsieur Etienne takes charge, walking up to the gate with an almost-swagger.

'You've kept us waiting far too long, Montgolfier,' Viscount Herges remarks coldly once he's let in. 'The few extra weeks you requested are over. Time's run out.'

'What about the sheep?' I ask. 'Didn't the Queen like her present?'

He glares at me. 'Of course she did. She's smitten with it.'

I catch Pierre's eye and smile.

'But,' Herges goes on, addressing the adults now. 'The King's anxiety has switched back to the English again. We've heard more from England: the air problem is as good as solved. So I've orders to take you directly to the King. If you can't get this flying device of yours finished here, then you're to do so under his supervision.'

Monsieur Etienne bows. 'I'm sorry for your trouble, Viscount.'

'It's the King himself who's gone to trouble,'

Viscount Herges replies irritably. 'Designers, seam-stresses, a whole team of workers await you at Versailles. With your designs, they'll get your invention made up in mere *days*.'

Monsieur Joseph, though, looks confused. 'Before we rush into anything—'

'*Rush?*' Viscount Herges snaps. 'You don't know the meaning of the—'

He catches sight of the laden up carts behind us. We step aside as he walks, trancelike, towards the great roll of balloon fabric.

'What's he doing?' Pierre whispers.

'Don't know,' I whisper back.

I certainly don't expect him to pinch the cotton between his fingers. Or to stare in amazement like he does.

'You've done it!' Viscount Herges gasps. 'I cannot . . . I've never . . . what I mean is, it's ready to fly, *non?*'

'We're doing our first test flight here, today,' Monsieur Joseph confirms.

'But with cotton *and* paper?'

'It's what we could afford and could assemble quickly.'

'Are you sure this will work? Is it not too fragile?'

'We've experimented with both separately,' Monsieur Joseph says, with a nod in my direction that makes me glow. 'Each has its merits, so this time we're trying them together. Though I admit silk would probably work best of all.'

Viscount Herges rubs his hands enthusiastically. 'This is indeed intriguing! I can't wait to see how it works in flight.'

Nor can we, I think.

He drops his voice. 'Afterwards, Monsieurs Mont-golfier, we'll return to Versailles together. You're to bring everything: plans, papers, notes – *everything*. We must make absolutely sure the English don't get hold of any of your resources!'

That glow I'm feeling? Stamped out. Gone.

'You've had word of spies?' Monsieur Etienne sounds anxious.

'Two of them at least,' Viscount Herges says.

I take a long slow breath. I should've known Madame Delacroix wouldn't work alone – she'd been quick enough to take me on, after all.

12

The demonstration in the marketplace is set for ten o'clock. A little after seven we head off for town, walking single-file alongside the loaded carts. It's Monsieur Etienne's idea that we dress to match the balloon's colours. So, Monsieur Joseph's wearing a blue frock coat and Pierre's in a red jacket that's already making him sweat. Monsieur Etienne is done up in *all* the colours – red coat, butter-yellow waist-coat, blue stockings. I'm torn between thinking him magnificent, and that he looks like an enormous parrot.

Even I'm given something new to wear. I'd have been happier in my maid's dress, but everyone insisted. So here I am in a blue gown, tied at the waist with red ribbon – except you can't see the ribbon because I'm carrying Coco in his sling. Madame Verte says it ruins the look but I won't leave him behind.

At first, the new dress makes me feel prickly and hot. I'm scared to move too much in case I rip it. By the time we get to town though, I'm glad to be wearing it. The red, blue and yellow of our clothes link us all together like a team or an army, and it's one I'm chest-burstingly proud to be part of.

The marketplace has been cleared for us. Judging by the church clock it's only a quarter to eight, yet already a few early gawkers are here to stare, which makes me get another flurry of nerves. Soon this place will be heaving with people, all here to watch us. I just hope we give them something worth looking at, something they'll remember for years to come.

Pierre and Monsieur Etienne get to work straight away, bashing four wooden posts into the ground to form an oblong. In the middle of it all the firewood is heaped. With Odette and Madame Verte joining us, we ease the balloon from the cart onto the cobbles and begin unrolling it. Again, I'm struck by its size. It'll take a lot of hot air to lift something this huge off the ground. We'll need one heck of a fire.

'Are there more logs?' Monsieur Joseph asks, stopping to wipe his brow. Out in the open, the pile looks worryingly small.

'That's all we've got,' Pierre replies.

Between them, they get the fire started. The wood's very dry, the flames hungry for it: I reckon on an hour's burning time, at most. We need more fuel. Monsieur Joseph sees it, too. 'The fire has to be bigger.'

'And hotter,' I add. 'Much, much hotter.'

'Bit late to realize that now.' Monsieur Etienne's mood is quickly souring. 'We haven't *got* more wood, and there's no time to fetch any.'

In the last half an hour, the crowd has swelled dramatically in size. Five hundred people or more now stand in the marketplace, many more leaning out of windows or climbing onto walls for a better view.

'We should've charged them to watch,' Monsieur Etienne remarks. 'Just a few coins each. Think of the money we'd make.'

The mood feels carnival-like, excitable, and incredibly noisy. Times like these are perfect for picking pockets, though today *I'm* the one slapping stray hands away, as people keep trying to touch our equipment.

'Oi! Stay back! Get off that fabric!' I cry for the umpteenth time.

Monsieur Joseph, flustered about the state of our fire, goes from person to person, asking if anyone has a woodpile nearby. All he gets though are shrugs and headshakes.

'We should've planned this better,' Pierre mutters. 'Is it too late to call it off?'

'Are you going to tell Viscount Herges, or shall I?' I say, nodding in the direction of the King's man who's watching everything at the very front of the crowd.

Pierre's right though; a bit more practice in the orchard beforehand wouldn't have been a bad idea. If we don't bring in more wood from somewhere, we'll never get this balloon up in the air.

In the end, Monsieur Joseph gives up asking for wood. We're going to have to work with what we've got, which is next to nothing. Our sorry little fire is gasping to stay alight. A team of townsfolk gather around the balloon to hoist it upwards. More people fasten each of the four ropes to the posts in the ground.

'All right, everyone! Stand by!' Monsieur Joseph cries.

Stand by for what? I think, frustrated. They can ready themselves all they like. It won't work without heat – proper, intense heat. And I bet Madame Delacroix is here somewhere in the crowd, writing all this down so she can share a great long list of our mistakes with the English.

A sudden breeze whips up the fire. Hot ash – a tiny whirlwind of it – falls on my new dress, burning through the fabric and making me yelp, though I'm more worried it'll land on Coco.

116

'Watch it!' I warn Pierre, whose red jacket is streaked with grey. All around us people are now patting their clothes and hair.

'Arrggh! I'm alight!' a woman cries.

'It's on your bonnet! Take it off!' The man next to her pulls it from her head and flings it to the ground.

More garments quickly follow. Hats, bonnets, even pairs of shoes come hurling through the air, landing very close to, even in, the fire. Some are smouldering, others are properly alight. There are jackets, waist-coats, a parasol.

'Keep 'em coming!' I yell, for I can see what's happening. As the pile of clothes grow, so do the flames. The heat, at last, begins to build. One thing's clear — the people of Annonay's clothes burn far better than their wood.

The balloon, no longer lying flat on the ground, billows, twitches, begins to rise. Through the opening at the bottom, the fire's heat pours in, making the shape fill up just like the undergarments did when hung over the stove.

Yet this is no petticoat. It grows and grows till it towers above us, an enormous, brightly coloured teardrop. It's a strange, remarkable, not-quite-real sight.

Now the balloon's full, it fidgets to rise higher. Still

tied down, the four ropes holding it over the fire stretch tight, the posts they're fastened to shifting in the ground.

I watch. Wait. Will it on in my head. Any moment now, any moment . . .

But Monsieur Joseph is cautious. He checks the ropes, the fire, makes notes in his book. He shakes his head at his brother, who's fretting and pacing.

'Come on, come on,' I mutter.

Though the bag stays tied down, it's fighting back, turning and twisting with growing strength. The crowd is getting restless. It's too hot this close to the fire; sweat pours down my back.

At last, when the balloon looks fit to burst, Monsieur Joseph raises one finger. It's such a little signal; I almost miss it. Though there's no mistaking the rush for the ropes. Nor the roar that goes up into the sky.

For a split second, the balloon hovers. Then it's off. It rises quickly above our heads, travelling across the marketplace.

'Follow it, Magpie! You're the fastest runner!' Monsieur Joseph cries. 'See where it lands!'

'*Oui*, monsieur!'

Ducking between legs, clawing past shoulders, I tear across the marketplace fast as I can. Everyone else is standing stock-still, heads back, mouths open. Even the boy midway through picking someone's pocket stops to stare at the sky.

At the crowd's edge, I slow down to check the balloon's progress. The balloon's risen fast in the last few minutes, its reds, blues and golds brilliant above the rooftops, looking for all the world like it'll never return to earth again. Watching, I feel myself grow lighter, as if part of me is up there with it, with nothing but the clouds for company.

If only.

When we checked earlier, the wind was a south-easterly. Now it's turned to more of a southerly, directing the balloon towards the river. Struggling to keep it in sight, I start running again. The street down to the river is shady, narrow. Twice I almost slip over. 'Sorry, Coco,' I say, because for him it's a bumpy ride. Shoes – even servants' ones – are useless for running in. In the end, I kick them off to go barefoot.

At the river's edge, I check the balloon's position again. It looks like it's lost a bit of height. The sky above Annonay bristles with church spires but luckily our balloon just about clears them all. Half-running, half-staring upwards, I keep following. As Annonay dwindles to a single shack and a pigsty, the balloon drops further. I'm hard on its heels.

By now the balloon is wrinkling. It looks less of a teardrop and more like an old potato. The air, the heat is seeping out. Already this flight's lasted far longer than any of the others, but I can't bear for it to be over yet.

'Just one more field!' I will the balloon on. 'Go on, you can do it!'

The balloon drifts over a wall. Over a field of sheep. Leaning heavily to one side, it's only twenty or so feet off the ground.

Scrambling over the wall, I force my legs onwards. The sheep don't look up – not at me, nor the huge cotton bag that lumbers past, just above their heads. In the field beyond though, someone is shouting. Two men in shirt-sleeves have stopped turning hay to stare in total amazement.

'What *is* it?' one of them cries. He's got his pitch-fork raised like the balloon's a wolf he's trying to fend off. I'm worried he's going to do it some damage.

'It's the moon fallen from the sky!' the other man gasps.

And fall it does. It hits the ground with a mighty thud. There's a rush of air as the fabric spills out, blasting me with dust. I reel backwards, shaken, spluttering.

Gradually, the balloon settles on the grass. All around it, the sheep carry on eating as if it's the most normal sight in the world. In his sling, Coco is fast asleep. To me, though, this is a thing of wonder. I feel proud and all choked up. It's taken weeks of preparation, bad tempers, secrets and experiments, but in the end the design *has* worked.

There's a crowd of people now striding up the field towards me, with Pierre, Monsieur Joseph and Monsieur Etienne leading the way. Their smiles are so huge I can see them from here. And who can blame them?

We did it. We made the balloon fly.

FOUR
FOR A BOY

13

Just after five o'clock, when the heat's leaving the day, everything is loaded onto Viscount Herges' coach. Versailles and King Louis await. It's the smartest vehicle I've ever seen – leather seats and windows you can open, pulled by four horses so white they must've been scrubbed. I'm still dazzled by what's happened today, and watching this latest part of it still feels like I'm in a dream.

'Chop chop, Magpie!' Madame Verte says, snapping me out of it. 'Fetch the last box down, will you? It's upstairs in the study.'

Instantly, I know which box she means. She doesn't need to tell me where to find it, either. I'm thrown into proper turmoil as I climb the stairs.

It's on the desk as I go in. The red leather is scuffed

and faded, the brass details old-looking. I run my fingers across it and before I know it, I'm checking if it's open. Of course it isn't: it's locked. As a box alone, I don't suppose it's worth much. But it's not the box that's important, it's what's inside.

Madame Delacroix will return, I know she will. And it comes back to me in a rush that surprises me because I've not had the thought again in weeks: would it be better for everyone if I gave her the box, after all? What harm could it do now? We're ahead of the English by days. The prototype is going to Versailles, with all the designers and helpers the King's hired, the Montgolfiers can probably get by without their notes. At least then, Madame Delacroix might leave us alone.

Glancing around the room, I see the study windows are open. It wouldn't be hard to believe a thief had climbed inside and taken the box. I could say it was a robbery, like the one they'd had before. When the Montgolfiers are gone, I'll slip out and find Madame Delacroix to give her the box to get rid of her once and for all.

It's not my finest idea but I've run out of any others. First, I need to hide the box, though, so I choose the small, unused bedroom at the end of the landing. Just as I reach it, Madame Verte calls up the stairs, 'Hurry with that box, Magpie! They're waiting!'

'Coming!' I shift the box onto my other hip. It's still as awkward as hell to carry, and heavy too, like they've packed every single notebook they've ever owned inside.

It's then the door to the next bedroom along swings open. In the doorway is a woman in a nightgown with a shawl over her shoulders. I almost drop the box in surprise. 'Madame M!'

She smiles. She's got Pierre's dancing dark eyes, though everything else about her is as frail as china.

'You must be Magpie,' she says. 'I've heard wondrous things about you – and your rooster.'

I feel a blush coming on. More so when Coco pokes his head out of the sling, which makes her laugh.

'You're going downstairs with that luggage, I take it?' she asks. Coming through the door, she closes it behind her, and before I know it she's tucked her thin little arm through mine. 'Help me, would you? I want to say a proper goodbye to my husband.'

There's nothing I can do but keep walking, the box under one arm, Madame M on the other.

'What are you doing out of bed?' Monsieur Joseph cries when we appear on the front drive. But he hugs her, carefully, of course. When they pull apart and she tidies his jacket lapels, I feel a lump grow in my throat.

The box is taken from me and put on the back of

the carriage, where already other boxes and baskets are piled high. The Montgolfiers' prototype, dusty but still in one piece, is at the top, covered in oilcloth. The red box is strapped up there too, balancing like a cherry on a madeleine.

And now everyone's milling around saying final goodbyes. Any minute the box will be gone.

Which is when the answer comes to me clear as day: never mind the box, it's me who should go. What if I vanish with it? That's the answer, and it'll be safer for everyone, wouldn't it? I'm only bringing trouble to this fine household.

I walk up to Monsieur Joseph, bold as you like. 'Can I hitch a ride to Paris, please, monsieur?'

He looks startled. 'Umm ... yes ... but ...'

'You've been so kind, taking me in and all,' I say in a rush. 'But it's time to move on.'

'Are you absolutely sure?' he asks.

'Yes, monsieur. This isn't my home and I've family in Paris I've been meaning to track down,' both are stonking lies.

Thankfully, the carriage is ready to leave so there's no time for second thoughts. I've nothing to take with me, just the maid's frock I'd changed back into earlier. Odette and Madame Verte say hasty, kind *au revoir*s. Pierre, though, is completely stunned.

'What's brought this on? I thought you liked it

here, Magpie!' Pierre cries, his voice wobbling. 'We need you. You're our lucky charm.'

'And you're mine,' I tell him. He's the only friend I've ever had.

'Time to go,' the driver announces, picking up his reins.

I give Pierre's arm a squeeze. It's easier than looking at his face.

As the Montgolfier brothers climb into the carriage, I offer to close the gate behind us. It feels odd walking down the drive one last time. A few months ago, when I'd crept down it in the dead of night, the plan was to be in and gone again, job done. It's peculiar how things work out.

Once the gate's shut, the carriage door swings open.

'In you get, Magpie,' Monsieur Joseph says from inside.

It looks a bit poky in there, to be honest, what with Monsieur Joseph and Viscount Herges crammed into one seat, Monsieur Etienne sprawled across the other. I can't see where Coco and I are meant to sit.

'We'll ride outside,' I decide, thinking it best.

The driver offers me a hand up to sit next to him. I take it, scrambling onto the narrow seat, which has a sort of sill where you put your feet.

129

'How long's the journey?' I ask.

'Three days and plenty more changes of horses,' he replies.

It sounds like a lifetime.

Once we join the main road out of town, the driver flicks his whip. And we're off. The horses race forwards with such speed, the force throws me back in my seat. Instantly, I'm regretting my decision to sit outside. Every stone, every pothole, sends my guts flying. What with holding on to Coco with one hand, and the seat with the other, I'm sure I'm hurtling towards hell. All I can think is: *three days of this?* I'll never make it to Paris alive.

Yet by some miracle, I manage the first twenty miles. And then, with fresh horses, the next twenty and the next. Each time we stop I prise myself off the seat and stagger to the ground.

The worst part of stopping is it gives me chance to think. I tell myself I've done right to leave Annonay. I couldn't stay with the Montgolfiers for ever – my past was always going to catch up with me in the end. At least this way the break is clean.

And to be going to Paris! What luck!

Except I can't get excited about a city I don't know. It'll be big, cold, nothing like Annonay. The coaching inns we've called at – rowdy, drunken places – remind me of life on the streets, the life I'm going back to. My heart is sinking fast. And if I think of the dearest friend I've left behind, I'm actually not far off despair.

Late the next night, we stop by a stream to water the horses, and I'm suddenly, violently sick. As we get ready to move on, the driver shakes his head. 'You ain't sitting with me.'

'I'm not ill,' I tell him. 'My guts just aren't used to carriages.'

'I ain't risking it. Ask them Montgolfiers if you can ride inside.'

But it's fresh air I'm wanting, not a cramped, stuffy carriage.

I take a weary breath. 'Where else can I sit outside?'

He jerks his thumb at the back of the coach where the luggage is, piled so high it's weighing the back wheels down. Top of the pile is the red valuables box; I can think of comfier things to sit on, frankly, and it must show in my face because the driver says, 'Your choice. It's that or walk to Paris,' which isn't a choice at all.

The swaying and bouncing's even worse up here. Eventually, though, I fall asleep and when I open my eyes it's nearly daylight. Down by my feet is the oilcloth, the one they've wrapped the balloon in.

From underneath it, I feel something move. Thinking it's a trunk coming loose, I lift a corner with my toe.

Hands shoot out to grab me by the ankles. There's a quack. Something feathery flies up into my face.

'What the—?' The shock nearly sends me overboard.

Voltaire lands on my lap. Coco, sensing him, lashes out with his feet. A human head and shoulders appear next. It takes a moment for my brain to catch up.

'*Pierre?*'

He's beaming from ear to ear like a halfwit.

'How long have you been there?' I gasp, glad *and* horrified. 'Since Annonay?'

He nods. 'I slipped onboard when you were opening the gate.'

There's no room for him to sit beside me, so he stays where he is. I hand him back Voltaire before there's a fight between the two birds.

'So no one knows you've come?' I ask.

'Not yet.'

He's looking awful pleased with himself too, but I'm worried for his poor mama. 'You should've told someone,' I say.

'You didn't tell anyone you were leaving,' he argues. 'You just decided and went – in minutes.'

'That's different,' I mutter. Doesn't he realize he's better off back in Annonay? I'd give my right arm –

and my left – for all that he has, for a family that cared where I was.

'You're not pleased I'm here, are you?' he says sulkily.

'Why *are* you here?'

'To go to Versailles, of course. To see the balloon flight. You must come with me, Magpie, oh say you will! Don't go to Paris!'

'But your papa doesn't know you're here.'

Pierre shrugs. 'It'll be a nice surprise for him.'

I'm not so sure.

Just then the carriage skids to a halt. We're on a country road, not a building in sight.

'What's going on?' Pierre asks.

'I don't know.'

We're at a standstill. Leaning round the side of the carriage, I call out to the driver. Then breathe in sharply. A man wearing dark clothes is standing in front of the horses, his lower face covered with a scarf. He's wearing a triangular hat on his head. Funny how I notice these details before I realize what's in his hand. It's a pistol, and he's pointing it at me.

14

'You, boy! Climb down at once!'
Glimpsing my short-haired head around the side of the carriage, it's an easy mistake to make, though I don't move.

'What's going on? Why've we stopped?' Pierre whispers.

'Stop asking questions!' I hiss. Truth is I've never been robbed before – it's always been me doing the stealing.

'Get back under the oilcloth,' I order Pierre.

'Where're you going?'

I lick my dry lips. 'I haven't decided yet.'

From the front of the carriage, I hear the driver yelp. Then footsteps approaching. I keep still. The footsteps stop as, with a clunk, the carriage door opens.

'Step outside, messieurs!' The robber's voice is rough, as if he's forcing it to sound that way. 'Hurry up. I've not got all day!'

The carriage rocks as Viscount Herges, Monsieur Joseph and Monsieur Etienne climb out.

'We have a little money.' This from Monsieur Etienne. 'Here, take my purse. I have a silver hat pin and there's a ruby in this ring.'

'Take them and let us be on our way,' Monsieur Joseph pleads.

'Not so fast,' the robber growls. 'I don't want your jewels. And keep your hands where I can see them.'

I catch my breath. There's one thing on this coach more valuable than rubies or silver — and I'm sat on it. The robber must be working with the English.

Footsteps approach the back of the carriage. At my left ear something clicks: the safety catch of a gun, I think, and feel a beat of terror.

'Perhaps you didn't hear me the first time,' the robber says.

Slowly, pistol still at my head, he moves to face me. It's my first proper look at him. I almost snort in surprise: why, he's not even a full-grown man!

I still haven't moved, either.

'Are you completely stupid?' the robber asks.

With his gun at my head, I know I've no choice but to get down. I do it slowly, mind, making it clear

I'm not happy.

'Well, well. Not a boy, after all,' he says, as I land in front of him. His gaze flickers over my dusty frock. He's got bright blue eyes, I notice, and blond hair that's escaping from his hat.

'I'm as quick and tough as any boy,' I tell him.

'Excellent, then you can start by unloading this luggage.'

There's no way to do so without revealing Pierre. Or the valuables box. Fiddling with the luggage straps, I make myself look busy, though really I'm buying time. The robber is twitchy, looking up and down the road. From the side of the carriage, I hear movement. The noise gets the robber's attention.

'I told you to wait—'

Monsieur Etienne comes at him like a giant bear. The force knocks the air from the robber's chest in one big gasp. They fall to the ground. Then Monsieur Joseph joins in. And Viscount Herges. I can't believe it. Neither look like they've had a brawl in their life, but suddenly they're rolling, grunting, cussing, all four locked together in one big heap. I try to get a punch in, but they're moving so fast I can't take aim. What worries me most is the robber's pistol: he's waving it dangerously at the carriage, the horses, the luggage pile, the sky.

'Come out slowly,' I whisper to Pierre. 'Take Voltaire

and Coco and hide up the bank behind the trees.'

Pierre does as I ask just as the four-bodied heap breaks apart. That pistol is really bothering me, though. It's still in the robber's hand. This time my kick hits home. Catching the pistol hard, I send it spinning high into the air. The robber yelps in surprise. The gun lands in a puff of dust some way up the road.

'Sit on him!' the driver cries, seeing the robber now disarmed. 'Don't let him reach the boxes!'

Yet before anyone can grab him again, the robber sets off after his gun. He's got the look of someone scarpering, knowing he's beaten. He's also holding his wrist, which makes me think maybe I kicked more than just the gun.

'Let's get moving before he returns,' Monsieur Joseph says, hurrying the other two men back into the carriage. He climbs in after them, leaning out again to speak to me. 'Magpie, please ride inside with us.'

'I will . . . just a minute . . . I need to . . .' I scan the bank, trying to find Pierre. Typical. I told him to hide, not vanish from the face of the earth.

'For heaven's sake, get in!' Monsieur Joseph cries, still holding the door open.

I can't. Not without Pierre. 'I'm coming,' I tell him, 'but Coco and—'

Gunshot.

My heart stops. The robber's hit someone, I think in panic. Who? *Who?*

Yet when I see him he's some way up the road. Gun recovered, he's fired into the air in a sort of frustrated show of strength. He does it again, then steps off the road, disappearing between the trees.

The gunshots have terrified the horses. I hear the driver up at the front saying, 'easy now' as they fidget and prance. The carriage jolts back, then suddenly lurches forward, making the door slam shut with a bang.

It's enough. The front horses rear straight up. There's a squeal, the driver shouting 'whoa!' as the air fills with dust. By the time it clears again, the carriage is careering down the road.

'Wait!' I yell, waving my arms above my head. 'Waaaaaaaait!'

Which of course is the very moment Pierre chooses to show himself, a bird under each arm. 'Sorry, I was just . . . oh!'

We both stare helplessly after the carriage. Already, they're so far away there's no point even trying to catch up. As for the robber, he's vanished completely.

Furious, I turn on Pierre. 'Where *were* you? Why didn't you come?'

'Ask him.' He pushes Coco back into my arms. '*He* took one look at Voltaire and ran off.'

'You were meant to be looking after them both!'
I cry.

'I tried! It's not my fault if your bird's a . . . chicken!'

'He's a ROOSTER!'

We glare at each other for a long, hard time.

I'm the first to speak, too desperate to be angry any more. 'Well, the horses have bolted and the robber's legged it. So it's just you and me. We've no money, no food, no water. And Paris is miles away on foot.'

Pierre's looking over my shoulder.

'Are you listening?' I ask.

'Magpie,' he says. 'What's that?'

He's pointing at something lying in the road. It's hard to see anything for dust at first. Then I see it. It's a box – *the* box – looking even more battered now, having tumbled from the back of the carriage.

'How did it get *there*?' Pierre asks.

Just before the fight started, I'd loosened the luggage straps, hadn't I? I'd not had chance to tighten them again.

'It was me.' I admit guiltily. 'The robber wanted me to take down the boxes. I was trying to buy some time and—'

'I'm glad you did,' Pierre interrupts.

'What?'

'Remember Viscount Herges told us the King wanted everything? All Papa's notes, all his drawings,

139

everything? To keep it all safe from the English?'

I do.

'So if they turn up at Versailles without what he's asked for—'

'They'll still be able to fly, though,' I say, not getting his point. 'They'll remember what to do. Besides, they've got the prototype.'

'But the King won't want anyone else getting hold of our designs. His order was to bring all their notes to Versailles.'

'Maybe.' I dig a toe in the dust, uneasy again. And not just about Monsieur Joseph, who'll be in pieces if he thinks he's let down the King of France. Frankly, we're better off without this pesky box. Wherever it goes, trouble follows.

'It's obvious, Magpie,' Pierre says, a bit too excited-ly for my liking. 'We'll take the box to Versailles. Now you'll have to come with me, after all.'

I narrow my eyes at the road ahead. I don't fancy the walk to Paris. I fancy it even less with a heavy box to carry. But the other options aren't pretty ones. The incident with the robber has shaken me. We need to get these notes safely to Versailles as fast as we can.

'All right,' I agree. 'You grab one end of the box, I'll grab the other.'

We set off like that, and at first it's not too bad. We even see the funny side of our birds and their constant bickering. Voltaire insists on walking ahead like our leader. Coco tucks his head back in the sling as if he can't bear to watch.

I don't laugh for long, though. Every shadow, every sound now is making me start. Though I don't tell Pierre, I'm pretty certain we're being followed.

15

We end up walking through the night. When we stop, we sleep in shifts, though I'm too jumpy to rest for long. All the next day, we walk. And walk, the sun so hot it makes the road ahead ripple like water. The only thing to drink is what's left in the puddles, and as for food, when we find a cherry tree, we eat too many all at once. It gives us the most vicious gut ache. Even then, doubled up in a ditch, I keep my eyes peeled for the English.

By the time we reach the outskirts of Paris, its evening.

'At last! We made it!' Pierre drops his side of the box with a thump.

We stand on the roadside, dazed and blistered. The sight of the city sprawling before us is incredible. I've never seen anywhere so vast, with streets running off in all directions as far as the eye can see.

An enormous archway seems to be the way into the city; beyond I see buildings so fancy they could almost be palaces, or very large, expensive cakes. There are people everywhere – on foot, on horses, in carts. I wrap my feet protectively around the box. I'm not taking any chances after lugging it all this way.

So this is Paris.

I stare and stare, and still there's more to see. After Annonay, where every crooked rooftop jostled for space, Paris seems as planned as a painting. Perhaps life on the streets here wouldn't be *so* terrible. And imagine what it would look like from above, from a balloon!

'You think we'll reach Versailles tonight?' Pierre asks. He's worried: I bet his papa will be too, once he realizes the box is missing.

Trouble is, Versailles's still ten miles away along the road that heads west around the city edge, and I'm so exhausted I can hardly put one foot in front of the other. But the longer we've got the box, the riskier things are.

'Let's get on with it, shall we?' I agree. Only, as I pick up my end of the box again, I go all lightheaded.

'Whoa!' Pierre catches me as I sway.

'I'm fine,' I insist. But a day and night without proper food and my body's protesting.

'Let's get some supper and then decide,' Pierre says.

I don't have the heart to remind him we're penniless.

Once through the archway, we soon discover another Paris altogether. This one isn't planned or beautiful but smelly and noisy, full of old timber-framed houses and people shouting in the streets.

There are stalls selling cakes and pastries, cheeses and bread. Some look delicious, some have been out in the heat all day, though I'm too hungry to care about the details. It comes back to me straight away, that twitchy, urgent feeling. In these crowds, thieving'll be easy.

Alongside a group of people watching a man with a dancing dog, is a stall selling fruit pies. I make a beeline. Pierre, on the other end of the box, gets dragged along with me.

I ask the seller for water. 'It's for my poor brother, see,' and I point to Pierre. The seller glances over my shoulder. That split-second look is all the distraction I need. A flick of my finger sends two pies tumbling off the stall's edge into my hand. Stepping back, I rejoin the crowds.

'What did you do that for?' Pierre cries, once we reach a quieter bit of the street.

I offer him a squashed apple pie, but he won't take it.

'You stole it, didn't you?'

''Course I did. I've got no coins. Nor have you, so

here,' I offer him the pie again, 'Eat it.'

He folds his arms. It's not in Pierre's nature to refuse food. He's doing it to make a point, I know. It's pompous of him. And it annoys me.

'Don't be an idiot,' I tell him. 'You need to eat.'

'You should've paid for those pies,' he says stubbornly.

'*You* need to stop acting like we're still in Annonay,' I snap back.

'Am not.'

'You are. Madame Verte isn't here anymore to make your meals so if you don't want to starve—'

'That doesn't make stealing right, Magpie.'

'Well, I'm not wasting them.' I cram his pie into my mouth straight after my own.

'Right, that's it,' he announces, and before I can stop him, he strides off down the street. Voltaire waggles after him.

In seconds, the crowds swallow them and I'm too weary to go after them. Proper fed up, I drag the box off the street, push it against a wall, and perch on top of it. Pierre'll be back in a minute, I convince myself. He won't go far without me.

I wait.

An hour or two passes and Pierre doesn't return. I can't believe he's been so pig-headed, stomping off in a grump in a place he doesn't know. He's bound to

145

get stupidly lost.

As it grows dark, I stop being angry and start to worry. Something's happened to Pierre, I'm sure of it. He's been robbed. Or beaten. Or both.

Up and down the street cafés light their windows and put chairs and benches out on the cobbles. The sounds of the city change. A man and woman argue somewhere. Cats squawk. A violin plays sad music. There's the spit and hiss of frying meat. Something hangs heavy in the air, something moody and danger-ous that makes my shoulders tense and I clutch Coco tighter to me.

I don't see the boy coming. It's his voice that makes me spin round: 'Can I help with your luggage?'

In a flash, I hook my feet tight around the box. 'Why? Who's asking?'

The boy's in spotless breeches and a smart powder-blue jacket that he's wearing loose like a cape over his shoulders. He's too well dressed for this part of town. I'm suspicious. He senses it too.

'Dear me, I'm not a thief you know.' He makes a good show of sounding offended. 'I was just passing through, and thought you looked in need of help.'

I don't believe him. Coco doesn't either. He aims a sly peck at the boy's arm. He misses. Just. The boy takes the hint, though, and moves back.

'I'm waiting for my friend. He'll be along any

moment,' I say.

'Perhaps I should wait with you,' the boy replies. 'It can be rather lively here at night.'

'I'd worked that one out already,' I mutter. Turning my back, I make it clear I'm not in the mood for making friends. Nor have I shaken off that sense of being followed. It's easiest not to trust anyone. I tap my foot, impatient, wondering where the heck Pierre is. I'm going to crown him when he finally turns up. Until that happens, I'm hoping the boy will get bored and clear off.

No such luck. He's persistent. So I end up telling him straight. 'Go away, will you? I don't need your—' I stop.

Ambling up the street in his shirt sleeves is Pierre. Voltaire's sat proudly on his shoulder. I detect a bit of swagger about them, which makes me want to wring both of their necks. I don't of course: I jump up and down with sheer relief.

'Oi! Over here!' I cry, flinging my arms around Pierre when he reaches me. 'Where have you been? Are you all right?'

'I'll be fine if you don't throttle me, Magpie,' Pierre laughs. 'Who was that you were just talking to?'

I turn round just in time to see the stranger boy walk off. So much for him offering to carry my luggage — under his jacket, his right arm is in a sling.

16

Pierre, meanwhile, pulls a fistful of coins from his pocket. 'See, I'm not a complete buffoon.'

In a shot, I cover his open hand. 'Flash your coin about like that and you won't have it for long!'

'Sorry!' He puts the money away. 'But I mean it, Magpie. We're eating supper tonight – one that we can pay for. Then we'll find a place to stay.'

'D'you hear that Coco?' I say, ruffling his feathers. He's still tense from our little encounter with the blue-coated boy. It's not helped that Voltaire's reappeared looking smug.

'Extra bread for our poultry,' Pierre confirms. 'As much as they can eat!'

I'd planned to be cross with him for leaving me for so long, but I can't help smiling. 'Where's this money come from?'

'I, my dear Magpie, sold my jacket and a silver buckle from my shoe.'

'What about the other buckle?' I ask, glancing at his feet. 'Didn't you sell that one?'

'That's tomorrow's food.'

I nod, impressed: he's learning. Hunger changes how you see things. A silver buckle isn't fashion, it's food in your belly, a bed for the night. And truth told, those fruit pies have done little to curb my appetite.

Picking the box up between us, we walk along the street until it joins another, busier one. Pierre chooses a café with steep steps leading down to a cellar. Inside it's dark and hot, with candles stuck in bottles on tables. By Pierre's standards it probably isn't up to much, but I'm thrilled. We find a seat in the corner, stowing the box and our birds beneath our feet.

Supper is whole spit-roasted chicken, best eaten with your fingers. Afterwards, Pierre declares it the finest meal he's ever eaten.

'Don't let Coco hear you say that,' I reply.

I'm sneaking bread under the table to two hungry beaks when I notice the group on the table next to ours. They're young people like us, laughing and thumping the table at jokes I don't get. Pierre does, though, and can't keep quiet.

'Excuse me, I think you'll find it's *vous*, not *tu*,' he

says to the person nearest us.

As the young man turns round, I groan out loud. Him again – the stranger boy. Except he's not quite a boy and not quite an adult; I'd guess he's about fifteen.

He recognizes me too. 'Ah, your friend returned, I see.'

I don't answer. As Pierre offers his hand by way of greeting I hiss frantically in his ear, 'That's who tried to help me in the street earlier. Don't trust him!'

Too late: they're already shaking hands. The stranger boy, I notice, does this gingerly though, his right arm is no longer in a sling.

'My name is Sebastien Delamere,' he says. 'Welcome to Paris.'

Pierre nods. 'Pierre, Pierre Montgolfier.'

I roll my eyes: this is just what we need: people knowing who we are. Boys acting like their fathers.

'And you are?' Sebastien turns to me.

'I think we should leave, Pierre,' I mutter, ignoring him.

But no one's listening to me anymore. Chairs are moved, cake is ordered and we find ourselves sitting at Sebastien's table with his friends, who all look and sound as expensive as he does. We jam the box between our seats for safekeeping.

'Keep your foot against it,' I whisper to Pierre. 'Don't say a word about what's inside it.'

Sitting Coco on my knee, I refuse to speak to anyone. What could I possibly have to say, anyway? I feel like I'm looking down on the world, watching everything from a distance. Girls like me don't belong with boys like these.

But after a bit I find I'm watching Sebastien. He speaks quickly, musically: people lean in to hear what he's saying. He smiles a lot too, and it is, I admit, quite a nice smile. Perhaps he isn't so bad. Maybe I just don't understand rich people.

Then I remember something.

'How d'you know we've just arrived in Paris?' I ask.

Faces, shiny in the candlelight, turn to look at me. Sebastien stops mid-laugh. 'What?'

'You said earlier, "welcome to Paris".'

'Did I?' he says, all breezy. 'I really don't recall—'

'You did.' I stare at him. 'How did you know?'

Someone coughs. I glance at Pierre, who looks embarrassed and says under breath. 'He was being friendly.'

'I'm doing my best to be,' Sebastien says. 'Anyhow, you're carrying that box around so it's obvious you don't live here, else you'd have left it at home.'

I catch Pierre's eye: *Don't say a word*.

'What's in it?' Sebastien rises out of his seat, craning to see between our chairs.

'Nothing.' I say. Heat spreads up my neck.

'Oh come on, it takes two of you to carry it – it must be heavy.'

'It's only papers,' says Pierre. 'Nothing very exciting, I'm afraid.'

'Don't tell him!' I snap.

Pierre holds up his hands. 'I hardly think—'

'He might be an English spy!' I blurt out.

Sebastien, eyebrows raised, points to himself. 'So I'm a *spy*? Is that what you're suggesting?'

Around the table, his friends laugh uneasily; a glare from him and they stop.

'You think I'm a spy?' he says again. He's not smiling any more.

'You might be,' I mutter. 'How are we to know?'

With a look of disgust, he turns to Pierre. 'Do you agree with her?'

'Well, no, I—'

'Someone must've put this idea into her head,' he interrupts. 'I can't imagine she'd have the wit to think it up by herself.'

'Being poor and dark isn't the same as being stupid,' I tell him.

Sebastien ignores me. He's now locked onto Pierre.

'You offend my honour, *sir*.' He stares at Pierre, who's gone visibly pale. I'm not sure why when I've heard far worse curses on the streets. But the others at the table share a meaningful glance, sort of horrified and excited.

'Why're you all looking at each other like that?' I demand. 'Pierre's done nothing wrong. I'm the one who called you a spy, Sebastien, so you leave my friend alone.'

Sebastien's response is to whip a leather glove from his pocket and slap it down on the table. His friends draw in one big sharp breath. Poor Pierre looks ready to faint.

'Tomorrow, Monsieur Montgolfier,' Sebastien says, 'You'll give me the satisfaction of meeting at the south entrance of the Tuileries Gardens, by the wall, at dawn.'

Out in the street, Pierre turns on me. 'You idiot, Magpie! What did you go and say that for?'

'What did I do?' I cry, exasperated. 'For all we know he could be a spy! Anyway, you were the one who mentioned the papers.'

'But it was what *you* said that caused offence. Don't you ever think before you speak?'

'He was pestering me earlier, wanting to help carry the box! And what about his arm, the one in the sling?'

Pierre tuts in irritation. 'He wasn't wearing a sling.'

'Not when you saw, no. But he was earlier – on his right arm – the one he'd probably use to hold a gun.'

'What are you talking about?'

'Think about it.' Now I'm angry too. 'There's been talk of spies for weeks back in Annonay. On the road we get robbed by a blond-haired, blue-eyed boy, then another one turns up in Paris and is unusually friendly.'

'You think *that* was Sebastien?' From the look Pierre gives me he clearly doesn't.

'It's possible,' I mumble, though the doubts creep in when I remember how the robber wore a scarf over his face. Just like I'd done, in fact, when I'd broken into Pierre's house, and he'd not recognized me.

'*Mon dieu!* You've no proof! You can't just accuse people! What you said to him . . .' Pierre splutters, '. . . why couldn't you have kept quiet?'

Dropping his side of the box, Pierre takes a long breath through his nose. He picks up Voltaire, who's flapping about worriedly, and tucks him under his arm.

'Magpie,' he says, trying to stay calm. 'You know what all this means, don't you? You know what Sebastien's just said?'

'Which part of it?'

He rolls his eyes. 'You don't know, do you?'

I didn't.

154

'. . . *the satisfaction of meeting* . . .' Pierre puts on Sebastien's silky voice, but somehow it isn't funny. 'He wants to fight a duel. I've offended his honour.'

I stare at him in disbelief. 'But *I'm* the one who offended him.'

I know what a duel is. Not that I've ever seen one, but I've heard stories of men shooting each other or fighting with swords. These aren't messy, drunken, scraps like the ones I've seen aplenty in the streets. It's how rich people settle their differences. And with a horrible, sickening realization, I see what trouble I've stirred up.

'Let me go back to the café and explain,' I plead.

Pierre shakes his head. 'Leave it. It's me he wants to fight. I'm a boy, you see, of a similar class. That's how it works. If I don't fight then I'm a coward. My reputation is ruined.'

'Didn't know you cared about your reputation.'

'It's not a joke, Magpie!' Pierre is fierce. 'Tomorrow at dawn I'll go to the Tuileries Gardens. I have to accept Sebastien's challenge.'

'But it's just stupid name-calling. You can't risk your life over *that*.'

Yet no amount of arguing or begging will change his mind. This stubborn side of his character is new to me. It's like shouting at a locked door.

'Whatever you say, it should be me fighting him,' I

say miserably. 'I was the one calling him a spy.'

Pierre sighs. 'Girls don't fight duels, Magpie. Not even ones with short hair.'

He's wrong about that.

FIVE

FOR SILVER

17

The wall in question is tall and made of stone: the next morning, true to his word, Sebastien is waiting beside it. He's got a friend with him, a boy I recognize from last night, who's carrying a small grey case under his arm. The city's clocks haven't yet struck four.

'Well, well,' Sebastien says, with a graceful bow of the head. 'I assumed cowardice would get the better of you, Monsieur Montgolfier. Clearly I was wrong.'

I bite my lip: he *is* wrong. More than he knows. With my nose and mouth well hidden behind a makeshift scarf, I plan for it to stay that way.

Monsieur Pierre Montgolfier is two miles away across the city, locked inside a little room above a baker's shop. He didn't plan to be – when renting it last night he supposed he'd be the one meeting Sebastien Delamere at dawn — but I'd woken first. The rest had been easy. Before he could even sit up, I grabbed Pierre's breeches and hat, and jammed the door shut behind me with a chair. He yelled to be let out, and I did feel mean, especially as I'd left him in sole charge of the valuables box and two grumpy birds. But they were all better off angry than dead.

And though Pierre's shoes are too big and his breeches too long, I make a pretty convincing boy. Standing here now though, the easy part is over. I'm going to have to fight like a gentleman's son.

The friend is called Olivier. We follow him over a locked gate to a far-flung corner of the gardens where the grass grows meadow-deep. The air, still damp with night, makes gooseflesh prickle up my arms. Or maybe that's fear.

Quite suddenly, we come out into a clearing. The grass here is flatter, shorter, stretching about one hundred yards in one direction, sixty or seventy in the other. Just the sight of it makes me shiver with dread.

Olivier calls over his shoulder. 'What do you think of our field of honour?'

I stay silent, shaking. Sebastien, walking ahead of me, tenses a little. 'Yes, it'll serve.'

Trees surround us on all four sides: just beyond them lies a whole teeming city, though you'd hardly know it. The leaves and branches soak up most of the sound.

This is the moment I make up my mind: I'm not going to die here, hidden away like an embarrassment. Mind you, it's easier *thought* than done.

Halfway across the grass, Olivier stops and with a click, opens the grey case.

'Your weapons,' he explains. 'First choice goes to Sebastien,' and he presents the case to his friend as if it's a fine meal on a platter.

Sebastien reaches inside the case. He takes out a silver pistol. I'd been hoping for swords or something that might not kill you outright. Then the case is in front of me.

'My father's duelling pistols,' Sebastien tells me. 'It's an honour today to use them.'

There it is again – that word, 'honour'. Personally, I can't even remember my father's face. His name might've been Amir, but I couldn't swear to it.

It's a million miles from how things are for Sebastien and Pierre. At the merest sniff of threat to their families they turn from gentle young men into something wild-animal fierce. I don't think I've ever felt like that about anyone apart from my rooster. I'm way out of my depth.

'Can't we just . . . I don't know . . . use swords or something?' I stutter.

Olivier looks at me like I'm lily-livered. A coward. I'm also a boy with a rather high-pitched voice.

So, wiping my sweaty palms, I take my pistol from the offered case without another word. It's surprisingly heavy with a long, pointed barrel. Though Sebastien seems to be checking his, I don't know where to start. Tutting, Olivier takes it from me. A few clicks, a catch flicked and he hands it back.

'That's the safety catch,' he says, pointing out a little lever above the handle. 'You'll want it off when we start.'

I nod.

Then he indicates a spot on the ground. 'If you start right here it gives you both twenty paces. One shot each. First shot goes to Sebastien.'

'Ten paces,' Sebastien argues.

Olivier gives a nervous cough. 'At ten paces your aim will be much more accurate so it's likely you'll—'

'That's the idea,' he snaps. 'This scoundrel called me an English spy, remember?'

'A single shot at ten paces could easily kill,' Olivier replies. 'I don't see how—'

'Ten it is,' I interrupt. Above us, the sky is turning light. We need to get this finished.

Olivier doesn't look happy. But he beckons to us both, making us stand back to back. There's a moment of quiet. I feel Sebastien's breathing, the warmth of him. I hope he can't hear my galloping heart.

Then Olivier says, 'Begin.'

Sebastien sets off one way; I go the other. To my left, Olivier counts our strides.

'Ten . . . nine . . . eight . . .'

Trying to ignore the churning sensation inside me, I focus on the pistol, cool and heavy in my hand.

'Seven . . . six . . . five . . . four . . .'

My strides are longer than usual: Sebastien's, I guess, will be shorter.

'Three . . . two . . . one. Stop. And turn.'

We turn to face each other. As I fear, Sebastien's still too close. So close, in fact, I see the way his necktie trembles at his throat. He's nervous too.

'First shot to Sebastien,' says Olivier, stepping backwards.

I breathe deep. Trying desperately not to move, I make myself look ahead at Sebastien. He stands, feet apart, his pistol in both hands. Raising it to shoulder level, he narrows his eyes. Then, he turns sideways, clicks off the safety catch, and raises the gun again, this time one-handedly. The barrel is pointing at my head. A strange calmness comes over me, as if this is happening to someone else.

'Fire!'

Something hot whizzes past my ear. There's a nasty, bitter smell. Smoke curls from the end of Sebastien's pistol. Hands on hips, he kicks the ground. 'He moved! The little pest *moved*!'

'One shot each you said,' Olivier replies. 'Now it's Monsieur Montgolfier's turn.'

Realizing what's happened, that Sebastien's shot has missed, I almost grin. The relief doesn't last.

'Monsieur Montgolfier, are you ready?' Olivier asks.

Shifting Pierre's hat back so I can see better, I raise my pistol like Sebastien did and plant my feet firmly on the grass. With a click I lift the safety catch. Turn sideways.

'Fire!'

Aiming at a spot to Sebastien's right, I try to steady my hand. But I'm not ready.

'Fire!' Olivier says again.

I focus on Sebastien's face. At the very last moment, I move an inch to my left. I squeeze the trigger. The gun roars. It bucks so hard I can't hold it any longer. It falls to the ground with a thud. Smoke hangs in the air. Though it's hard to see anything, I can hear Sebastien's not happy.

'It was a dumb shot,' he protests. 'Montgolfier didn't even *try* to hit me.'

He's right; I didn't. As the smoke clears enough for me to see his furious face, I fear I've probably just made things worse for myself.

'Two dubious shots do *not* satisfy my honour,'

164

Sebastien says. 'I demand another attempt.'

Olivier glances between us, bewildered. 'But you said one shot each.'

'*Proper* shots, yes. Not half-hearted attempts.'

If there are actual rules for this duelling lark, then it seems they're the ones people invent to suit themselves. Already, Sebastien is checking his pistol again. That done, he walks back to his spot.

'I really don't think this is a good idea,' Olivier warns.

Sebastien ignores him. His eyes are blazing a strange, bright blue. The safety catch clicks off.

I hold up my hands. 'Look, I've said I'm sorry. I don't want to fight any more. Can't we just stop a moment and—'

The shot cuts me short. I hear whizzing. A force like a punch hits my head and sends me reeling. Pierre's hat spins to the ground.

He's shot me!

I wait for my legs to buckle. Any moment I'll be lying down, looking up at the sky for one last time. I'll never say goodbye to Pierre. Or Coco. This is it.

Gingerly, I touch my forehead, which I'm expecting to be wet with blood and brains. There's a lump there, all right, but I'm surprised to find it dry. My legs crumple anyway. I yank the scarf off my face, suddenly needing air.

This time, as the gunsmoke clears, I hear laughing. Or perhaps I imagine it. I'm not sure what's real. Then I see Sebastien striding towards me. I cower, fearing more pistol shots. But he's looking at me with a sort of stunned delight.

'Magpie!' he cries. 'I can't believe it! It's you!'

Still dazed, I let him clap me on the back like a long-lost friend. I've no idea what I've done to deserve it. Yet as I gather my wits again, I learn something else about duels: the one factor more important than winning is courage.

'You faced two pistol shots!' Sebastien gushes. 'Two! I'm in awe!'

'*One* shot,' I remind him. 'You said the first was a dumb shot which was why we've had to do it all again.'

That seems forgotten now. The way Sebastien looks at me so admiringly makes my stupid face redden.

'You've done all this for your friend Montgolfier! What a lucky fellow he is.'

'I don't know about that,' I mutter.

'Indeed, it's true. You've defended his honour and proved your own.'

'He didn't have much choice. I shut him in our room.' I pluck at Pierre's breeches. 'And I stole his clothes and all.'

Perhaps it's shock or the fact I'm still alive, but suddenly I've a bad case of giggles bubbling in my throat. Catching Sebastien's eye, we start laughing. We're doubled up, holding our ribs like they'll break if we don't, and when we're done I think, at last, we might be friends.

18

fterwards, Sebastien and I walk back across the city. The early sunshine is already turning hazy. It's going to be a hot, sticky day, and breeches, I'm learning, are not as cool as skirts. I'm also reminded, once again, that there are people – as well as poultry – I care about in this world. Life's not just about looking out for yourself.

'Shall we stop for breakfast?' Sebastien says as we pass a chop house opening its shutters.

At the mention of food, my stomach growls.

'Let's fetch Pierre first,' I decide, knowing he'll be hungry too.

As we arrive at the baker's where we took rooms last night, Madame Petit the owner leans out of an upstairs window. 'Oh Mademoiselle! Thank goodness you're back!'

Moments later, she's downstairs, rushing through the shop doorway.

'It's the boy. He's gone!' she cries. 'A man came for him and ... oh ...'

'Who came?' I'm taken aback.

'They left so fast in a cart ... Oh that poor child – and in his nightshirt, too!'

I glance guiltily at Pierre's breeches.

'Slow down,' Sebastien says calmly. 'Now, tell us again.'

But Madame Petit can't get her words out.

'Was it Pierre's father?' I can't think who else would fetch him away. 'Did the man have a bald head? Or – hang on – he might be wearing his wig?'

All she does is shake her head and sob.

I've a queasy feeling this is about the box. Pierre was right all along to think Sebastien wasn't behind any of the theiving attempts. How could he be when these past couple of hours he's been with me?

Which makes me think again of that nasty piece who held up our coach. Or the sense I'd had of someone trailing us along the main Paris road: if it wasn't Sebastien, who was it?.

Leaving Madame Petit, I race up the stairs to our room. Sebastien's right behind me. The mess that greets us stops us both in our tracks.

'Heavens above!' Sebastien gasps.

I'm lost for words.

There's no door – it's been smashed to pieces. A window's broken too, glass all over the floor. The bed's on its side, the chair thrown across the room, a chest for clothes wrenched open. Everything's been rifled through, fast and furious.

It's not just Pierre that's gone, either. The birds are missing. There's not even a feather left behind. I shake my head, distraught.

'Who could've done this?' Sebastien asks.

I glance at him sideways, the old suspicions flaring up. But he doesn't look like he's pretending. His jaw's clenched with anger.

'The *English*,' I say bitterly. 'They've been after us right from the start.'

They haven't taken the box, though. It's still here on the floor, the lock torn apart, the lid open. All that's left inside are ink stains and a dead wasp. There's a tear in the paper lining. The notebooks, of course, are gone.

Despairing, I bury my face in my hands. If I'd been here when the Englishman came Pierre and I would've fought him off together. But I wasn't here, was I? I was fighting an argument *I* started. The horrid truth is that I've let Pierre down so badly I don't deserve him as a friend.

'You look as if you need to rest,' Sebastien says.

'What I need,' I insist, looking up, 'Is to go after Pierre, as quick as I can.'

'We don't know where they've gone,' Sebastien points out.

Squishing my eyes tight shut, I try to think of where the Englishman might take a boy in his night-shirt with two pet birds in tow. But all I picture is Coco stiff with terror, and Voltaire sulking, and poor Pierre begging oh-so-politely to be freed. It just makes things worse. If they're travelling by cart like Madame Petit says they really could be anywhere by now.

'Do his family live nearby?' Sebastien asks. 'I don't wish to alarm you, Magpie, but he has been abducted, so we really should let his parents know.'

I unsquish my eyes. 'Versailles – that's where his father is. We were supposed to be going there anyway to deliver this box.'

Sebastien stares at what's left of the valuables box on the floor. 'Are you going to bring it with you?'

'No point,' I reply. 'They've taken what they wanted.'

He looks about to say something, but thinks better of it. 'Versailles it is then. If you hurry you might just get there before the weather breaks.'

Glancing out of the window, I see what he means.

The sky's turned a flat, hazy white. There's not a breath of wind. In this tiny, smashed-up attic room, it feels hotter than ever.

'Not on foot I won't,' I reply. 'I'll have to get wet.'

'I have a horse,' Sebastien offers.

I think it over. I'm not completely sure of him, even now. He's a bit *too* nice. A bit *too* well-dressed. I don't know how to *be* with people like Sebastien. Life was simpler when his sort were just a pocket to pick.

'I can't ride,' I tell him.

He smiles his twinkly, sunshine smile. 'But I can.'

We go straight to the back street where Sebastien's horse is stabled. I'd imagined a smart courtyard attached to his family's house, but this is just a row of stalls next to a coaching inn. The whole place runs alongside the river. In this heat, the smell coming off the water – night soil and rotting fruit – makes me want to gag. It's an odd place to keep a horse, especially for someone like Sebastien.

The horse, though, is magnificent. He's a huge, gentle grey named Dante, who pricks his ears at us and makes a whiffling noise when you say his name. Sebastien acts fast. Before you know it, Dante is saddled up ready and we're both on his back. Sitting astride him is like doing the splits. I'm glad of these breeches, after all.

We leave Paris at a brisk trot, Sebastien in front, me behind clinging on for dear life. After the pot-holed city streets, the road to Versailles is straight and flat, lined on either side by poplar trees. There isn't much traffic either so Sebastien pushes Dante into a canter.

At first I'm too terrified to look, though after a mile or two of the horse's smooth rhythm, I decide it's safe enough to relax a bit. Another couple of miles, and Sebastien tweaks the reins to slow Dante to a trot, then a walk. The poor creature is caked in sweat.

Swinging his leg over Dante's neck, Sebastien jumps down. I catch him clenching and unclenching his hand like it's stiff.

'Are you hurt?' I ask.

'Of course not.' He brushes it off. 'Dante needs a breather, that's all. We've still got four or five miles to go.'

I peer up at the darkening sky. 'Looks like we're going to get wet after all.'

Sure enough, it begins to rain. Steadily, the drops get bigger, pock-marking the dust on the road. The thunder overhead makes Dante flick his ears, which I've heard means a horse is nervous.

'Don't worry,' Sebastien says, as I grip the front of the saddle. 'It'll take more than a thunderstorm to scare him.'

No sooner are the words out of his mouth than a

huge white flash lights the sky. A beat later the thunder comes, so loud it makes the air hum. Dante goes tense beneath me. His head disappears between his front legs, he twists, kicks his back legs, throwing me onto his neck. As his head swings up again, he leaps forward, tearing the reins from Sebastien's hand. I don't scream. I'm too terrified to even unclench my teeth. Grabbing handfuls of mane, I sit tight as Dante takes off.

'For heaven's sake, pull the reins!' Sebastien yells.

How he expects me to do that I've no idea. I can't even let go of Dante's mane. Careering from one side of the road to the other, he's completely out of control. The rain blinds me. I'm slipping sideways on the wet leather. I don't know what to do, but I can't hold on much longer. I'm going to die of panic, or be sick, or fall off into the road, whichever one of these fates gets me first.

SIX

FOR GOLD

19

Amazingly, I don't die. I don't fall off, either, but my stomach's set up camp somewhere in my throat so it's lucky we didn't eat that breakfast Sebastien promised. As the road begins to rise, Dante settles into a steadier gallop. I unknot my fingers from his mane enough to grab the reins, though pulling on them doesn't make the slightest difference. We go on like that for miles – me pulling, Dante not taking any notice. And then, at a sudden bend in the road, Dante swings left, plunging down what's little more than a muddy country lane, where he spots a tasty patch of grass. Next thing he stops sharp, puts his head down to graze. And I go whizzing straight over the top. I land in a messy heap in a hedge.

I'm covered in mud and bits of twig, but nothing's

broken. Dante's so filthy he doesn't even look grey any more but at least neither of us is injured.

In every direction, all I see are fields. And trees. I've a sinking feeling we're completely and utterly lost. How I'm going to find Monsieur Joseph I've no idea, never mind tracking down Pierre.

Seizing Dante's reins, I try to pull his head up. 'Stop eating, greedy guts. We need to get back to the main road.'

The horse, as seems to be the way of things between us, ignores me completely.

'Come on, Dante – *move!*'

From the direction of the hedge comes a giggle. I turn round. I can't see anything – the hedge is thick – though from behind it something rustles.

'He's not very good with horses is he, poor thing,' a woman whispers.

'Ssssh!' hisses another. 'He's spotted us!'

There's more giggling. It's starting to irk me.

'If you think you're so clever, you come and move this horse!' I snap.

Silence. Then a snort. Then a massive hoot of laughter and two ladies' heads appear over the hedge.

'Do forgive our shabby manners,' the one with dark hair says. She sounds rich like Sebastien. 'I expect you know your own horse better than we do.'

'He's not mine,' I say. 'He's my friend's, who I've lost.'

'Oh dear. Would you like us to move *the* horse?'

I'm not sure if she's teasing still or trying to help.

The other lady – fair haired, pretty – nudges her. 'We can do better than that, Gabrielle. Let's ask the poor boy to tea.'

I shake my head. 'I can't—'

'Oh, let's!' This Gabrielle person is all bouncy like a puppy. 'I've never taken tea with a poor boy before, and I'm *very* sure you haven't, Marie.'

She pushes against part of the hedge, which swings open like a hidden gate, and the two women come through it to my side. They're wearing these flimsy white dresses, the sort that milkmaids wear except they're spotlessly clean as if they've never been anywhere near the underneath of a cow.

'You don't understand.' I try to say. 'I've lost my friend – actually *two* friends. I've not got time for tea.'

'Everyone's got time for tea,' Gabrielle replies.

Bold as anything, she takes Dante's reins from me and leads him back through the gate. He goes with her, too, meek as a lamb.

'You can't take him!' I cry. 'He's not mine! I need him!' But she's already disappeared.

Now I'm really stumped. The fair-haired woman – the one called Marie – slips her arm through mine. 'Don't look so glum. We have three different types of cake for tea.'

179

I could stand here and argue. But tea and cake isn't exactly the worst thing that might happen. And it dawns on me that these women in their funny too-clean dresses might know the way to Versailles. So I go with Marie, thinking I'll stay just for the cake then make my excuses and leave.

Passing through that gate though is like stepping into a made-up world. We cross a field that looks more like a garden, and through gardens that look like magic. There are bushes clipped into bird shapes, roses twisting over walls. I smell lavender, mint, see peach trees and apple trees sagging after the rain. We pass water fountains carved out of gleaming white stone. Everything's beautiful – a bit *too* beautiful. The colours and smells make me dizzy. All the while, I'm trying to remember our route so I can find my way out again.

Eventually, we reach a cottage with a thatched roof and timber walls, and even that looks more like a doll's house than a real one. It's incredible that these women live in such a perfect place when Paris, with all its stink and bustle, is just a few miles down the road.

Gabrielle's arrived ahead of us. She's setting up a table outside the cottage with a snowy white table-cloth and dainty teacups and spoons. To my relief, Dante's tethered to the fence and munching on hay. Another animal is here too, tied to the table leg by a length of pink ribbon; from what I can see of its curly white rump it might be a dog. As soon as Marie sits down she reaches under the table to stroke it.

'Have a seat.' Gabrielle pulls out a chair for me.

I sit down. Then the cake appears, and there really are three types – cherry, honey, strawberries and cream. As I eat, Marie feeds titbits to the dog under the table, while she and Gabrielle bombard me with questions. Have I ever used a fork, they want to know. Can I read? Do I have more clothes than the ones I'm in? It's a bit off-putting to be honest, like I'm a curiousity from the fair.

When I can get a question in myself, I ask the quickest way back to the main road.

'Where are you going?' Gabrielle replies, stifling a yawn.

'To Versailles.'

A look passes between them. Then, in the bush to our left, something moves.

'Oh no,' Gabrielle mutters under her breath. 'Here we go.'

And just like that the whole bush is suddenly a frenzy of arms and red-trousered legs.

Two men come crashing towards us, swords raised, yelling, 'Keep away from the Queen!'

I'm mightily confused.

Gabrielle rolls her eyes. 'Calm down, everyone.'

'King's orders, your Majesty.'

The men are guards. I feel a twist of panic as his words sink in. *King's orders*? Could this mean I'm nearer to Versailles than I'd thought? Why is he telling me to keep away from the Queen? And who's he calling '*your Majesty*'?

The guard doing the talking has an enormous ginger moustache. 'We've to arrest any strangers on the estate, especially anyone who might be English,' he says, gawping at me.

'He's just a boy having trouble with his horse,' Gabrielle explains.

'Aha!' Ginger Moustache says. 'But how do we know he's not spying for the English, eh?'

'I'm honestly not!' I tell him, nervous now.

Gabrielle tuts. 'Tell them to stop this nonsense, Marie.'

As Marie clears her throat, the men bow. Just slightly. And suddenly it becomes clear: *she* is the Queen.

I stare so hard I think I forget to blink.

Marie, the person who's just poured my tea and cut my cake, is Marie Antoinette, the Queen of the whole of France!

I can't believe it, not when she's so pretty and so gentle in her manners, yet in the news-sheets they make her seem like a greedy monster. How's it possible that she's the same person?

If this *is* the Queen then she's not looking very sad, either, despite what the King's letters said. I'm hoping that's down to Lancelot, that our gift really has cheered the Queen up, though sitting here in her fairy tale garden, I've got my doubts. Would a grubby sheep sent all the way from southern France really do the trick?

It's then that the pet dog under the table stomps on my foot.

'Ouch!' I cry.

'Don't move!' the guard warns. He lunges forward, lifting the cloth with the tip of his sword. He's holding his breath like he's expecting a tiger to leap out.

'Oh for goodness' sake,' Gabrielle snaps. 'It's a sheep, not a spy!'

I sit forward, very eager to see this *sheep*.

Sure enough, with a yank on the pink ribbon, Gabrielle pulls the creature into the open for the guard to see. It totters out, blinking and chewing cake.

It's not Lancelot, I'm disappointed to see. *This* sheep is so white it looks like a cloud on legs. Realizing it's not a spy, Ginger Moustache lowers his sword in relief. I decide this is a good time to slip away. Yet when I get to my feet, the guard's sword is up again in a flash.

'Sit,' orders the guard. 'I'm not finished with you yet.'

Frustrated, I sit again and try explaining. 'Please, I need to find the Montgolfiers to tell them about their son. He's been taken by an English person against his will.'

The Queen looks astonished. 'The Montgolfiers *are* here at Versailles, yes. There's to be a demonstration in a few days' time over the Palace! We've invited half of France to watch their flying machine! Won't it be incredible?'

'That useless pair?' Gabrielle laughs. 'There's more chance of that pet lamb of yours flying, Marie, than the Montgolfiers getting anything off the ground!'

Which proves just how little she knows, I think crossly.

'Where will I find the Montgolfiers?' I press her. 'I need to speak to them.'

But the Queen's turned to Gabrielle. 'I've had an entire wardrobe of new dresses and shoes made for the occasion. Louis doesn't know yet. I haven't told him.'

'You naughty creature!' Gabrielle cries, clapping her hands in delight.

'You'll have to help me decide what to wear, *cherie*.' And the Queen starts reeling off all the hats and shoes and frocks she's got to chose from. I think she's forgotten we're even here until the guards cough politely.

'If it's the King's orders then you'd better take him,' she says with a waft of her hand, then goes back to discussing dresses.

I grit my teeth: now *this* is more like the Marie Antionette from the news-sheets, dismissing me like I'm a bit of stale cake.

But before I can protest, I'm hauled away so fast I can hardly keep up. I'm tripping and stumbling and sick with frustration.

'Just listen, will you? I'm not a spy. Or English,' I say more than once. I'm not a boy either, though they're still convinced of that, too.

'We've already got your friend, son,' Ginger Moustache says. 'So save your excuses.'

I scowl at him. 'Friend?'

The guard, liking his little bit of power, won't say any more, which leaves me eaten up wondering which friend he means.

20

The moment the Palace of Versailles comes into sight, my feet slow down: it's hard to walk and stare at the same time. To call it a house is like calling the Queen 'Marie' – the word's too small to fit it. I thought the houses on the Montgolfiers' street were fine, but this is something else. It's completely and utterly jaw-dropping.

We approach from the front, up wide steps into a courtyard. The walls on every side are full of windows and gold-coloured balconies, all sparkling so much it makes me squint. I'm marched round the back to what I guess is the servants' entrance. Somewhere inside are the Montgolfiers, I keep telling myself. All I have to do is find them. They'll know what to do about Pierre. We'll track down him and the birds, and everything will sort itself out. It's hard to stay hopeful though with a guard hanging off each arm.

We don't go inside, either. After walking the whole length of one side of the Palace, we're now facing a steep grass bank. Set in it, small and rusty and out of keeping with how grand everything else looks, is a door. Or rather a hatch, bolted shut.

One guard opens it, the other holds onto me. We're hit by a waft of damp, underground air. I panic.

'I'm not English!' I insist for the umpteenth time. 'Just take me to the Montgolfiers, that's all I ask!'

'Save it, sonny.' Ginger Moustache goes through the hatch, pulling me with him. It's all I can do to stay on my feet.

Inside is a passage with lanterns hanging on the wall. Ginger Moustache takes one for extra light: I soon see why. Up ahead, the passage becomes steps that take us deeper and darker underground. I try not to think of all the earth and grass above our heads, or the doors or windows that aren't here. And I definitely don't think about the sky.

At the bottom of the steps, we turn right into another tunnel. My heart is knocking away in my chest, too fast for my liking. Another few yards and we reach a door, the top part of which is all bars. The key to unlock it is the size of a dagger.

'In here.' Ginger Moustache pushes me inside. The room smells of cold and earth.

'You've got this all wrong,' I tell him desperately. 'I need to speak to Monsieur Joseph Montgolfier!' He ignores me, but he does at least leave his light.

The door closes. I hear the awful sound of the key grinding in its lock. Even with the light I can't see anyone else in here. So much for a friend: the cell looks empty but for me.

I wrap my arms around myself. I don't know what else to do. I'm stuck.

At some point I notice something shuffling through the straw on the floor. Rats, most probably. There's no obvious ways out for any living thing: no hatches, no secret doors, no loose stones in the wall. This cell is lock-tight. Frustrated, I kick the straw.

QUACK!

'Oh!' I leap back in surprise.

The *quack* comes again, a proper telling off that can only mean one thing. Swinging my light towards the noise, I'm suddenly all hope.

'Voltaire? Is that you?'

Something larger than any rat waddles across my feet. I laugh out loud. 'It *is* you!'

A stride away, I find Coco. He's a sorry state, mind you, keeping his head tucked under his wing.

'Coco,' I plead. 'Come on, it's only me.'

As I pick him up, his little heart's going *boom boom boom.*

'Shh!' I whisper, trying to calm him though I'm feeling savage because if that Englishman who took him has laid so much as a *fingernail* on my bird, I'll ... I'll ...

'Watch where you're walking, Magpie!' The weary voice is Pierre's. He's just to the left of the door, slumped against the wall. The light's enough for me to see his puffed up right eye, the split on his lip. It's a shock – and a mighty relief – that he's at least in one piece.

'What happened?' I cry, rushing over. 'How come you're here?'

'Let's just say I had a visitor.' He tries to smile about it, but winces instead.

'Back in Paris, you mean?'

He nods. 'A man came – nasty type, he was, with a terrible French accent. He went for the box, but I wouldn't let him have it.'

I think of the smashed-up door, the upturned bed. Poor Pierre. I should've been there with him.

'But the man took what was inside the box?' I ask.

'He did, though he wasn't very happy about it. Don't think he expected to have to kidnap us, either. He kept complaining about it being all too much for one person.'

'Did he bring you straight here?'

'Yes.' Pierre winces as he sits more upright. 'He had to meet someone, apparently.'

I remember what Viscount Herges said about a pair of English spies at work together, and I'm back to thinking about Madame Delacroix again like I can't shake her off. She's in on this, I pretty certain.

'We got stopped at the tradesman's gate,' Pierre tells me. 'The man pretended to be a carpenter, until Voltaire quacked.'

'Good old Voltaire.'

Pierre looks pleased. 'He couldn't speak much French, either. The guards didn't trust him after that.'

'Sounds like they caught one real Englishman at least,' I remark. 'And the notebooks? What happened to them?'

'I don't know. We got marched off so quickly my feet hardly touched the ground.'

I know what he means about that. I'd also be happier if we knew for certain where those notebooks are.

'At least you're alive, Magpie,' Pierre says. 'I had visions of you shot to pieces by that *rake* Sebastien.'

'I shouldn't have left you. It wasn't a decent thing to do,' I mutter, so awash with the guilts I can hardly meet his eye. Even fighting the duel doesn't seem a fair excuse any more. It was stupid to leave him alone with the box.

'How did you find us?' Pierre asks.

'I wasn't exactly looking,' I say truthfully. 'We came to tell your father you'd been taken, and—'

'*We?*'

'Sebastien's got a horse. We rode here from Paris and—'

'Sebastien *helped* you?' Pierre interrupts, astonished.

'It's all right. We're friends now.' For some reason, saying this makes me blush.

'I'm so glad to see you, Magpie,' Pierre says, and my guilts for leaving him get ten times worse until I see he's pointing at his breeches. 'I'll have those back now, if you please. You can keep the shirt.'

Fair's fair. I do as he asks, and as the shirt-tails hang down to my knees it's almost as good as a dress.

After we've swapped clothes there's little else to do but sit. And wait. My brain doesn't get the message, though. It's churning and whirring, cogs in a wheel. There's lots of this that still doesn't add up. Why was the man with Pierre coming to Versailles anyway? Why would an English spy bring the notebooks *back* to their owners? Surely he'd be desperate to smuggle them away to England as fast as he could?

And what of the Montgolfiers? If their notebooks don't turn up in time, will they really remember enough of the process to make the balloon fly again?

I don't know. And I'm not likely to find out, stuck

in this prison cell. Even the birds can't be bothered to squabble. We're all as gloomy as each other.

'How long d'you think they'll keep us here?' Pierre asks.

I shrug. 'You have tried to tell them you're a Montgolfier, I take it?'

'I haven't, no.'

'What?' I turn to face him. 'Why the devil not?'

'Think of our family name,' Pierre tries to explain. 'It'll look terrible for Papa. At best they'll think he's a father who can't control his son. At worst, they might think we're *all* spying, Papa and Uncle Etienne included.'

'So we just have to sit it out, do we?' I protest. This is getting more bewildering by the second.

'I was caught sneaking into the palace with an Englishman,' Pierre reminds me. 'It looks pretty suspicious.'

I slump back against the wall. So we're definitely stuck then, aren't we? I've got this dreadful feeling we'll be here until the flight is over – at least.

'It's funny to think they're convinced we're spies though, isn't it?' Pierre ponders. 'I can't even speak English, for goodness sake!'

Funny isn't a word I'd use right now.

'They're not taking any chances with anyone,' I reply, and leave it at that.

There's no point trying to explain Madame Delacroix. Or how this tangled-up mess started with five gold coins on a back street. The Magpie Pierre believes me to be – I like that girl. I don't want it to change.

We fall quiet, then. I shut my eyes in the hope of catching some kip. Inside my shirt, Coco's already snoring. At last, when I'm almost drifting off, voices start up outside our cell. It's two men speaking. I prop myself up on an elbow to earwig.

'The King wants to see which ones are the best weight,' says First Voice.

'Sounds like he wants to eat them,' Second Voice replies.

They laugh. It's not a nice sound.

'He might as well eat 'em,' says First Voice. 'If the machine doesn't finish them off the shock of it will.'

There's a grunt of agreement from Second Voice. ''Tis playing God, making people face their deaths like that.'

I sit bolt upright, pretty sure they're talking about the Montgolfiers' balloon.

A key scrabbles in the lock, the door opens. I'm on my feet in a flash, helping Pierre onto his.

'Grab Voltaire,' I tell him, holding Coco extra-tightly. If anyone tries to snatch our poultry again, I'll bite and kick as good as a mule.

There's more than two guards here. I don't see exactly how many but the cell feels suddenly smaller. They have lamplight. Lots of it. The cell fills with it, too. Then sudden, confusing dark as the light moves around. I start backing away from people I can't even see.

'Listen,' I say, hands spread in front of me. 'You've got this wrong. Pierre's a Montgolfier and he—'

'Ssssh, Magpie! Remember what I said! Keep quiet!' Pierre hisses in the darkness.

I hear feet — lots of them — swishing through the straw towards us. Then someone has hold of me.

'Pierre?' I call out. 'Are you still there?'

'Get walking, boy,' says a man's voice close to my shoulder. 'This machine won't wait for ever.'

The fear all coiled up inside of me is unravelling. I start to doubt what I'm hearing because that word — 'machine' — doesn't fit right. What we made back in Annonay we called 'le balloon'. Before I can stop myself, I'm suddenly picturing that other machine, the one invented by a doctor that's in all the news-sheets with its big wedge of a blade, dripping with blood. The machine that cuts off people's heads in one clean chop.

21

We're marched out into daylight, then inside again and through the Palace. The guards surround us – five up front, five behind, two either side – like we're dangerous criminals and they're not taking any chances. Over shoulders, between knees, I glimpse gold ceilings, white marble floors, chandeliers the size of carriages. This place is so bright it's like walking into the sun.

The guards are going too fast. But when I drag my feet to slow us up, all they do is lift me by the armpits and carry me. It's agony. Soon I'm pleading to be put down again, but they don't.

Pierre tries another tack. 'Please, gentlemen,' he says politely, though he's as flustered as I am. 'This has got rather out of hand.'

I wonder if he's thinking of the head–chopping–off machine too. He certainly looks scared.

The guards aren't listening. We keep moving. We take a left turn. A right turn, going so fast I lose track of which way we're heading.

Soon the corridors start to look the same – gold and marble everywhere, paintings of ugly men and plump-faced women and fruit the size of cannon-balls. I feel lost, as well as scared. Pierre's wincing again, holding his side. I'm worried he won't keep this pace up much longer.

Then the corridors turn darker and plainer, with stone floors and a smell that makes me think of chamber pots in need of emptying. We go through a huge scullery, past a row of sinks where maids, their backs to us, scrub away in silence. A door then takes us out into a cobbled yard. The Palace walls crowd in on all sides but at least the air's fresher out here, and above us is a square of sky; instantly I feel better. It's even more the case when, finally, the guards put me down.

The machine is here.

Not a head-chopping-off one, thank *everything*. But a weighing machine, over by the kitchen steps. It's a big one – as tall as a man, I'd say, with a sticky-out brass arm where the weights are slid along. It's just like the ones they use in Annonay marketplace to measure grain.

'You weighing us or the birds?' I ask.

No answer.

The guard in charge I recognize as Ginger Moustache. Earlier he'd given me his light, so I'm a tiny bit hopeful: he won't let anything *terrible* happen to us. *Will* he?

'Is this to do with the balloon?' I want to know.

Ginger Moustache talks over the top of my head. 'We'll start with the taller boy. Bring him over to the scales.'

Still no one's said why they're weighing us, either. Just as he's about to step onto the scales, Ginger Moustache demands Pierre hand over Voltaire.

'Don't you *dare* take his bird!' I barge at the wall of men around me. It's so solid I bounce off again and stumble back.

'And while you're at it, take that chicken off the darker boy,' Ginger Moustache growls, pointing at me. 'We want these weights to be accurate.'

'He's a *rooster*,' I tell him. I don't give in easily, either. Nor, I'm pleased to see, does Coco.

'Argggghhh!' one of the guards cries, 'it's bitten me!'

There's a decent amount blood on his knuckles too. But then another guard seizes Coco from me, and despite my yelling and kicking, won't give him back.

When Pierre's finished on the scales it's my turn. They make me stand very still, which is hard because my legs are shaking. It doesn't help that the guards take ages, fiddling with the weights and looking thunder-faced like something isn't right.

Finally, it's done, the results are written down.

'Right,' Ginger Moustache barks. 'Let's get these *John Bulls* upstairs to the King.'

The guards close in around us again. I stuff my hands into my armpits, not wanting to be hauled along like last time. On tiptoes, I try to look for Coco but can't see him, or Voltaire.

'You haven't given us back our birds,' I tell Ginger Moustache.

'Forget the birds. You're the ones the King wants to make fly,' he replies.

'*Us?*' I stare at him like I've not heard him right. Then at Pierre, who's gone a grubby shade of white.

Ginger Moustache nods. 'Criminals. English people. He won't risk a French life but he'll happily risk yours.'

I almost laugh. Us, go up with the balloon? Does he mean it? Could that *really* happen? Hadn't Monsieur Etienne said that they'd not put people in the balloon? Hadn't that been how he'd persuaded Monsieur Joseph to keep going? It's a change of heart, all right. But I'm suddenly giddy because it makes perfect sense: *this* is why we've been weighed.

Before I can ask more questions, we're hurried out of the yard as fast as we entered it, and back along the same stinky corridor. This time though I'm tingling with excitement.

'Don't you see?' I hiss to Pierre, who looks like he's just lost his last coin down a drain. 'This could be incredible! We could be the first people in history to fly!'

Pierre gives me a withering stare. 'We're also prisoners, Magpie. There's nothing "incredible" about that.'

I'm torn between thinking he's just being a misery guts and thinking he might be right. Surely it's worth pretending to be English – until the flight, anyway – if it means we get to go up in the balloon.

'What about Coco and Voltaire?' he whispers. 'Don't you care what's happened to them?'

'Of course I do!' I'm annoyed he's even asked, but I don't know how we're going to get them back.

We're heading upstairs again, each step taking us further from our birds when, turning a sharp corner, we stop dead.

We're facing a different set of stairs now. Coming down them is another group of people. They're mostly men, a few women. There's got to be twenty of them, all with that ragged-to-the-bone look I know too well. Like us, they're surrounded by guards.

As we wait for them to pass, Ginger Moustache catches me staring.

'They're more of your lot – English spies,' he tells me proudly. 'Been rounding them up all morning, we have. The place is crawling with them.'

I tuck my chin in, scowling. He can't mean it. They can't all be English spies – that's just stupid.

'Then England must be half empty at this rate,' I mutter to Pierre.

He's not listening. Beside me he's gone as tense as a cat.

'That's him,' he says under his breath. He's staring at one of the men on the stairs. A tall man, ratty-looking, with a long neck and hair that coils around it in a thin ponytail.

'Who?' But from the knot in my gut, I guess: this is the man who kidnapped Pierre, who smashed up the box and took the papers and our birds.

He's seen us now too – or rather, Pierre – and hesitates for a second on the stairs. I lick my lips. I'm ready for him.

Just as he approaches, Pierre steps in front of me. It's as if I need protecting or something, which I don't. The guards are milling about. There's suddenly too many people, a muddle of red trousers, swords, thin bodies.

And Pierre, who I realize isn't protecting me at all.

He's trying to give me something, to push it into my hand. I don't know what it is, but I snatch it from him quick, just as the long-necked man's arm snakes through the crowd and grabs Pierre's sleeve.

'Give it to me!' He snarls in his funny accent.

Pierre pulls back. The man makes a lunge for Pierre's throat. He gets nowhere near it though. The guards push him down the corridor in the opposite direction from us. We're taken on up the stairs.

'Phew!' Pierre says. 'That was a bit close!'

Now I'm the one barely listening. I'm staring at what he's just given me.

22

I don't suppose for one second Pierre's turned into a thief. Yet the object he's stuffed into my hand – almond-shaped, with a swirly pattern on it – is heavy. Good metal. I bet it's worth a fortune.

'Move it you two!' a guard orders.

In panic, Pierre gestures for me to hide it. I'd rather he took it back again, but I don't have much choice. Pretending to itch my leg, I tie a knot in my shirt hem and hide the thing inside, where it'll have to stay for now.

Up on the first floor, we're taken into a room that's so eye-poppingly huge it's easily the size of the Mont-golfiers' orchard back home. At first I don't see the people seated down the far end; the guards do though, because they stop to salute.

Pierre breathes in sharply. 'Magpie! It's King Louis and Marie Antoinette!'

I gulp. No sign of the Montgolfiers though. Perhaps we're not going to be flying anywhere after all, except back to our prison cells. I try keep my cool. Easier said than done, mind you, when you're being marched right up to the King and Queen of France.

They don't notice us, not even when we stop in front of them. They're too busy having an argument – a right old barney by the sounds of it – which makes them seem so normal, I have to swallow down a nervous giggle.

'*How* much?' the King is saying. He's done up to the nines in a wig and a cheerfully bright waistcoat. Shame his face is so grumpy.

'I can't remember,' the Queen replies. She's dressed up too – wig, powder, beauty spot, the works. Frankly, she looked prettier before when I met her in the gardens. The gleaming white sheep is with her, still wearing a ribbon round its neck like a leash. It's busy nibbling the buckles on her shoes.

'More than the cost of running your little farm?' the King asks grimly.

The Queen sticks out her bottom lip. 'You wouldn't begrudge me a few new frocks, would you, Louis dearest?'

Ginger Moustache coughs politely. You'd have to

have your head in a bucket of sand not to notice us by now. They keep bickering, though, ignoring us completely. At some point my gaze wanders to the sheep.

She's familiar, all right. And now I see her properly, it's obvious. The sheep is Lancelot! My heart does a cartwheel. I can't believe I didn't recognize her before. The nibbling's the giveaway — it's the very thing she used to do to my bare feet.

'Lancelot!' I mouth, willing her to look my way.

She carries on nibbling, so I try a sneaky little click of the tongue. Nothing. Not so much as a flick of her ears. She's forgotten me already. Sad though I am, I'm glad things have worked out well for her. Shame I can't say the same for poor Voltaire or Coco. Or us.

When the King finally addresses us, his temper is proper sizzling.

'You took your time, man!' he barks at Ginger Moustache. Then he points his walking cane at us. 'These are the spies, are they?'

'Indeed they are, your Majesty,' Ginger Moustache mutters, like he's already apologizing for us. 'The best I could find.'

I stand very straight. Chin up. Eyes front. The King of France can think what he likes just as long as he puts me in that balloon basket.

'Good grief! Look at the size of them both!' the

King rages. 'I bet the bigger boy weighs as much as a pony!'

Pierre gasps, offended.

'Montgolfier said no more than forty pounds in weight,' the King goes on. 'You *were* listening, weren't you?'

'Indeed I was—'

'They need to be smaller!' the King insists.

'But these *are* the smallest of the prisoners,' Ginger Moustache replies.

The King narrows his eyes at the guard. At us.

'Then we'll have to hack a bit off of them, won't we?' he says.

Ginger Moustache is aghast. '*Hack*, your Majesty?'

I don't dare look at Pierre. The Queen giggles into her fan, but something about the King makes me think he's serious, and suddenly I'm not sure even flying is worth losing a body part for. Ginger Moustache tries to splutter out an answer. He's saved by the doors opening behind us.

'Ah, there you are Montgolfier!' the King booms over our heads. 'Let us pray you have better news.'

Pierre and I spin round as Monsieur Joseph bustles in. His wig is all askew and there's ink on his fingers. It's enough of a shock seeing me — it stops him dead. Yet when he spots Pierre the colour completely drains from his cheeks. No wonder: the son he thought safely tucked away in Annonay is here at Versailles with a face full of bruises.

Monsieur Etienne blinks at us in total disbelief. 'What in the world—?'

I'm just glad to see them – a bit choked, in fact. Before I can even think of rushing over, Pierre grabs my shirt-tails.

'Remember what I said,' he whispers. 'We've got to pretend we don't know Papa.'

It's too late anyway. The guards close in and jostle us to the other side of the room.

It's Monsieur Etienne who catches my eye as he passes. Though I'm not expecting it, he winks at me. Just once. It gives me a tiny pinch of hope.

Now it's the Montgolfiers bowing before the King. Seeing them seems to calm his temper, thankfully, though I'm still anxious as to where this is going to lead.

'You've decided you want living passengers for the flight,' the King states.

'Yes, your Majesty, quite so.' Monsieur Etienne, confident as ever, does the talking. 'We want to study the effects of altitude on beating hearts and breathing lungs.'

'These two *criminals* will do,' says the King. He points at us again with his cane. 'I'm told they weigh over forty pounds but we could . . . *make adjustments*.'

I wish he'd stop saying this.

'Your Majesty,' Monsieur Etienne goes on. 'I'm not convinced of the merits of using *real* people at all. Not yet, anyway. We're not entirely certain of the safety . . .'

The King looks surprised. I'm not, though. After the accident with Pierre, this was always Monsieur Joseph's view.

'The flight might go wrong, your Majesty,' Monsieur Etienne explains. 'We're not yet completely certain of the robustness of our design.'

Or is this because of the lost box of notebooks, I wonder? Was Pierre right all along? Was I really a bit too hopeful to think they'd remember every detail? Possibly.

Or maybe the balloon's simply not ready — for passengers, that is — though I'd be willing to take the risk.

'Perhaps if we use something living that isn't a person? An animal, perhaps?' Monsieur Etienne suggests.

'An *animal*? What's the matter with you, man?' the King cries.

Monsieur Etienne keeps his cool. He's good at this: he could argue for France. 'Is it wise to put two suspected English spies in the balloon? Might that not lead the English to claim *they* are the first to fly?'

This hits home.

'Hmmm.' The King peers down his long nose at us. The look is cold, blank, like he's choosing which knife to use at supper.

'Find me an alternative, then, Montgolfier,' he says finally. 'And quick on it. Everything needs to be ready by sundown.'

Pierre's shoulders visibly drop with relief. The very idea of flying again terrifies him, I know, but I'm gutted our chance has gone. All we've got to look forward to is being sent back to our cell – without Coco or Voltaire – who by now could be in any number of savoury dishes.

'An animal that isn't designed to fly would be perfect,' Monsieur Joseph suggests. His gaze falls on Lancelot. 'Something like a sheep, perhaps.'

I'm alert again.

The Queen places a hand on her pet sheep's head. 'Then go and fetch one from the fields, Monsieur Montgolfier,' she says coolly. 'You're not having mine.'

I'm biting to tell her she needn't worry – from my days of tending Lancelot, I know she weighs *less* than thirty pounds, at least she did when I weighed her for the butcher. But the King is now looking at his pocket watch and yawning.

'Marie, I'm hungry and extremely tired,' he says pointedly. 'Let's not waste any more time. It's already past seven o'clock.'

'They're not having her.' The Queen, folding her arms, sits back in her seat.

Trouble is, the King's stubborn too. He closes his watch with a sigh. 'A favour for a favour, my dear. If you want to keep those new dresses of yours, I suggest you be a little more generous in return.'

And with that the Queen's face softens. She unfolds her arms, leans towards the King.

'Very well,' she says prettily. 'Though promise me it'll be in all the records, that the Queen's pet sheep was the very first living creature to fly.'

The King pats her shoulder: 'Of course, my dear.'

'And that we give her a proper, noble name.'

She's already got one of those, I want to point out, but the Queen has her own ideas. 'Something apt.' She pauses, thinking. 'Gabrielle had a parrot called Montauciel once,' she says, then glances at Pierre and I. 'Which, if you'd care to know, means "climb-to-the-sky" in English. I think that will suit very well.'

Without any more fuss she gives Lancelot – I can't think of her as Montauciel – to Monsieur Joseph. Nor could I imagine handing Coco over that easily, not for all the fine dresses in France.

Smug now he's won the fight, the King offers the Queen his arm as they get to their feet. If the King thinks he's solved the weight issue, I think bitterly, he's wrong.

'You'll need more than the sheep, your Majesty,' I say before anyone can stop me.

A dangerous hush falls over the room. Pierre gives me a warning kick to the ankle.

'Ouch!' I glare at him. 'It's true. Lancelot ... I mean the sheep ... she weighs less than forty pounds so ...'

'Your Majesty,' Monsieur Joseph cuts in, wobbly voiced and nervous-sounding. 'Rest assured. If the sheep alone isn't enough, we'll have to use other animals to make up the weight.'

The Queen flashes the King a look. 'What *other animals*?'

'No more of yours, my dear,' he tries to calm her, then to Monsieur Joseph. 'What did you have in mind?'

'As with the sheep, a creature that doesn't fly naturally – a chicken, perhaps,' Monsieur Joseph replies.

The King nods: 'Take whatever you need, Montgolfier. It's vital we get this right.' Then to Ginger Moustache with a sweep of his free arm, 'See to it that these men want for nothing. Anything – *anything* – they request, you do it. That's an ORDER!'

He barks out the last word so everyone jumps. Pierre, though, shoots me a hopeful look. He's thinking what I'm thinking – of Voltaire and Coco. That's if we're not already too late.

23

Even when the King has gone, the Montgolfiers still pretend they don't know us— there's no eye contact, no hugs, no 'what the devil are you doing here's. They're playing it extra-safe until the flight is over, and so must we; Pierre keeps hold of my shirt-tails in case I need reminding.

Ginger Moustache, meanwhile, is keen to get things underway. 'Allow me to escort you to the kitchens,' he says to the Montgolfiers. 'We'll weigh the sheep properly and find you some poultry, *ça va*?'

'It needs to be alive,' Monsieur Etienne reminds Ginger Moustache, as they leave the room. 'And healthy. No palming us off with something half-dead.'

I seize my chance. 'Please Monsieur Montgolfier. If you find an orange rooster and a white duck in the kitchens, please, *please* use them.'

Monsieur Etienne stops, raises an eyebrow. Monsieur Joseph looks back over his shoulder, his gaze darting to Pierre, then me. It's the briefest of looks. An even briefer nod. I just hope he's got the message.

The door to the King's rooms closes behind him. There's nothing more to be done now. The balloon flight will take place, the King will be happy, the Montgolfiers will get their names in the history books.

I'm trying to be hopeful.

This time tomorrow, when it's all over, the Montgolfiers'll come clean about who we are and we'll be freed from our festering cell. Until then we'll have to wait it out. Already I'm tapping my toes, grinding my teeth because this waiting lark might well be the hardest part of all.

A guard with tiny currant eyes is now in charge of us. He's spent the last few minutes out in the hallway talking to Ginger Moustache and the Montgolfiers. He comes back into the room, rubbing his hands with glee.

'Right you two,' he says. 'I've had my orders where to take you. Let's get you locked up again, shall we?'

My mood sinks as I picture the dark hours stretching ahead. What makes it crueller is knowing that, outside in the sky above our heads, the balloon will be flying and we won't get even the tiniest glimpse of it.

'Here goes,' I mutter to Pierre as we head for the stairs.

Yet instead of going down to the cells, the guards take us upwards. I'm totally thrown.

'Where are we going?' I ask more than once. Pierre does too, but as usual, they blank us.

Up and up we go, to the very top of the house, the attics. It's hot up here and just as stuffy as being underground. But at least the last of the evening sun is still shining in through the windows.

At the end of a long, narrow passage we finally stop in front of a door. The currant-eyed guard wrestles with a set of keys, whistling through his teeth till he finds the right one. The door opens onto what was probably once a servant's bedroom. It's low-ceilinged, dusty, with a bed and a trunk for storing clothes in; I've definitely seen worse places to spend a night.

'You've gone up in the world, you have,' the guard remarks, ushering us inside.

It's a bit of a shock, being spoken to finally, especially as he doesn't even sound that unfriendly. Behind us, the other guards wait in the passage. Though I notice their hands aren't on their swords any more. They're not exactly standing to attention, either, but leaning against the wall. The whole mood feels different, almost relaxed. I look at Pierre, who shrugs: neither of us have a clue what's going on.

'Why've we been moved?' I ask.

The guard considers me narrowly. 'You might as well know,' he says with a weary sigh. 'Monsieur Montgolfier demanded it. Said it wasn't right to put children down in the cells. What he wants, he must have. You heard the King himself say so.'

'Oh.' I catch Pierre's eye and smile, though he doesn't smile back.

'And while you're in here, find yourself some decent clothes.' The guard aims this at me. 'Shocked at the sight of you, Monsieur Montgolfier was. You should find a frock to fit you in that trunk over there.'

'A *frock*?' It's a bit of a jolt to be reminded I'm not a real boy. And good guesswork from the guard because, filthy and short-haired as I am, I don't look much like a girl.

Yet I think I understand. This is Monsieur Joseph's way, saying in a quiet manner that he *does* know who we are, and he's making sure we're all right until this is over. And I'm glad of it.

Pierre, though, still seems in some sort of grump. Once the guards have gone, I soon find out what's eating him.

'How could you offer Papa our pets like that?' he

cries. 'If that balloon isn't safe enough for people, it's not safe for Voltaire!'

'Whoa! Steady!' I hold up my hands in surprise.

'I'm serious, Magpie. You of all people should know the balloon will probably crash land. What happened to you was bad enough – imagine those injuries on Voltaire, or Coco, or Lancelot! It'd probably kill them!'

'You're being daft,' I say, not liking that he's got a point. 'It won't crash, they'll be fine.'

'Oh, you know that, do you? For certain?'

I glare at him. 'Well, they won't last the night down there in the kitchens. So at least I've given them a fighting chance.'

We're both upset and bristling. And when I think maybe Pierre understands what I've done, he soon puts me straight on that score. 'Don't look too smug, Magpie. We've still got to face my father and uncle when this is over.'

'*You* have,' I remind him. '*You're* the one who ran away. They're not *my* family.'

He gives me a look I can't quite read.

Later, we're brought supper – bread and broth on a tray slid inside the door by a guard's foot.

'You can have the bed,' I say to Pierre, once we've licked the dishes clean. 'I'll take the floor.' We're not arguing any more, but as the taint of it's still hanging in the air, I'm trying extra-hard to be nice.

'Thanks.' Pierre flops down on the bed. It sends up so much dust, we both start hawking and coughing. There's only one window – small, set in the eaves – and I don't expect it to open. But, with a stout push, it does. Mid-shove, I feel a sharp something digging into my thigh.

'Ouch!' It's the gold thing Pierre made me take from him on the stairs. What with everything else, I'd forgotten it. The window open, I set about unravelling the knot in my hem.

Pierre props himself up on an elbow, watching. 'I'd better tell you about the brooch, hadn't I?'

Holding it in the flat of my hand, I can see that's what it is. The almond shape is in fact a feather, the work on it so fine you can see every little line and detail. As I turn it this way and that, the gold catches in the late sunlight. In all my thieving days, I've never seen such a stunning piece. I can't take my eyes off it.

'It's . . . *beautiful*,' I say, because no other word will do. 'Where's it from?' There's a pause. I look up in alarm. 'You didn't nick it, did you? Oh Pierre, tell me you didn't!'

'No, I didn't steal it,' he admits. 'The Englishman was after something else inside the box, not just the notebooks, something hidden. But I got to it first.'

I frown. 'What d'you mean *hidden*?'

'He was searching the lining of the box. I saw him do it. Then he heard someone moving about downstairs and went to the door to listen, and . . .'

'. . . you found the brooch and pocketed it,' I finish, guessing the rest. 'It must belong to your father if it was hidden in amongst his papers?'

'I suppose so,' Pierre agrees. 'Though I've never heard any mention of it before, or seen my mother wear it.'

I stare at it longingly. 'I bet it's worth a bit. He probably wanted to sell it on.'

'Maybe.' He doesn't sound sure.

'What, then?'

Pierre sits up properly. 'When the Englishman couldn't find the brooch, he went completely, raving *mad*!'

I think of the room as I'd found it, chairs on end, the box all smashed up.

'I know this sounds stupid, Magpie, but it was as if the brooch meant more to him than the notebooks. He was in such a state he almost forgot to pick them up.'

'He's a spy though, isn't he? There's loads of them here, we saw them on the stairs.' To be honest, though, I don't know what to think. Perhaps the man just got dazzled by a fancy bit of jewellery. It *is* an amazing bit of gold.

'Put the brooch on, Magpie,' Pierre says suddenly. 'Go on. I can tell you like it.'

I grin, head on one side. 'Really? Should I?' and I'm thinking, *why not? It can't hurt.*

But first I'd better find something half reasonable to pin it to.

Taking the guard's advice, I search the trunk. It's full of old stiff fabrics and yet more dust. The frock that fits me best is made of blue calico. It's been inside the trunk quite some time because we find mice nesting in the skirts. Once I've tucked them safely back inside an old jacket, and shaken out the frock, it looks passable. *More* than passable when I've yanked it on and pinned the gold feather to the front of it, at the place just above my heart.

'*Voila!*' I say to Pierre. 'How does it look?'

'Like it was made for you.' He smiles, lies back on the bed, eyes already closing sleepily.

The brooch cheers up the plain calico no end. It cheers *me* up, too, to wear something so lovely and pretty and not, for once, be thinking how much it's worth or who to sell it on to. I almost feel a bit light-headed, suddenly. It's a nice sensation, like I'm about to be lifted off my feet.

Best enjoy it, I tell myself, because it's the closest I'm going to get to flying.

24

Just before dawn, I wake up feeling stiff and cold. This floor's not the comfiest I've ever slept on. Nor am I used to sleeping without Coco in the crook of my arm. I miss him. And I bet Pierre misses Voltaire too, though right now he's still asleep. When I remember what's happening today, the thrill of it hits me hard.

I'm fully awake and on my feet in an instant. The window, still open from the night before, lets in a draught that smells smoky. On eager tiptoes, I look outside. It's a beautiful morning. The weather is fine – clear blue sky, and sunshine so perfect it makes my blood sing.

After yesterday's round-up, I can't imagine any English spies left in the world to ruin things. So in a couple of hours' time when the balloon takes off, I'm going to enjoy it. After all, we're in a room with a great view of the sky.

Our animals will be fine, I tell myself. Better this than the butcher's block.

With a bit of heaving, I manage to climb out onto the roof. It's a good thing I'm not scared of heights. The rooftop's at least sixty feet off the ground and isn't flat at all. It's full of gutters and gulleys and more attic windows that pop out of the roofline like eyes in a toad's head. It's magic up here, our own secret world where we can see everything but no one sees us.

I look down.

Our window is slap-bang above the palace's central courtyard, and if I shuffle forwards on my backside I can see right over the edge. I can't believe our luck. From here we should even be able to see Coco and Voltaire being brought out for the flight. We couldn't have nabbed a better spot if we'd tried.

'Pierre!' I call over my shoulder. 'Get yourself out here! It's amazing!'

It's still quite early, yet down in the courtyard the final preparations are in full swing. Servants scurry about with trays, men on ladders put up flags and hang flowers. Hundreds of chairs have been set up around the fountain.

'Pierre!' I try again. 'Wake up or you'll miss Voltaire!'

Already the crowds are beginning to arrive. Carriages pull up, people come on foot. There's a long line of traffic all the way down the drive. This isn't Annonay marketplace: today is on a whole different, mind-boggling scale.

The balloon has to work.

Yet I'm suddenly struck by all the horrific things that could go wrong. The fire might spread. The balloon could crash into the crowd. Or what if it doesn't take off at all and the Montgolfiers are the laughing stock of France? If anything does fail there's tens of thousands of people to witness it. It'll be all over the news-sheets in no time.

It's not helping, thinking like this. I take a deep breath. English spies and stolen notebooks aren't going to ruin today. Even so, I do a quick scan of the light summer frocks and tall grey wigs in the crowd for a woman who'd stand out like a crow amongst this lot.

Behind me, a scrabble. A grunt. Pierre, awake at last, squeezes himself through the window. I pat a place for him to sit beside me. But he stays back, clinging to the window frame for dear life.

'No chance,' he says. 'I'm not sitting that near the edge. Not even for Voltaire.'

'You won't see anything from back there,' I plead, holding out my hand.

He won't have it, though. He won't even move. Just being up here is making him go a funny shade of green.

'Oh come on—'

He cuts across me, '*SACRÉ BLEU!*'

It makes me jump. 'What's the matter?'

He refuses to let go of the window frame even to point. But I see where he's looking, at a spot beyond the house, beyond the courtyards. Blocking my view in that direction is of a row of chimney pots, but when I stand up, I can see right over the top to the ground below.

At first, I think something's happened to the grass down there. It's not green. It's bright blue. There are patterns on it – gold ones. And this odd-looking grass runs from the courtyard edge all the way to the first set of garden steps.

Then I realize. 'Oh . . . my . . .'

'Exactly,' Pierre finishes. 'Isn't it incredible?'

What we're staring at is the completed balloon laid out flat, ready to be filled with air. No wonder the King hired so many people to help make it. This version is vast. It's not done in the Montgolfier's colours this time, but the King's own sky blue and gold. Every inch of fabric is patterned with leaves and cherubs and swathes of ribbons. It reminds me of the King's rooms where we met him yesterday: the paper on the walls looks just like this. Quite honestly, it's a work of art.

'Imagine what it'll look like in the air!' Pierre's starting to sound excited. *I'm* the one worrying now, about the fire they'll need to get this huge thing airborne, because it's a mistake we've made before. If the balloon comes down too soon, it'll mean the flight's a failure. If it drops too quickly, it'll put our living passengers at risk, and I don't dare mention that to Pierre.

I shift forwards for a better look at the preparations. There *is* a fire down there, that much I can see – and smell – it's where the smokiness I smelled earlier is coming from. So far, it's burning well. But it needs to stay that way.

'I just hope they've got enough fuel,' I mutter anxiously.

Pierre nods to the left of the fire. 'You have seen their woodpile, haven't you?'

I have now.

It's not a wood*pile*, it's a wood *mountain*. And still servants are coming with armfuls of logs, handcarts piled high with junk – fence posts, rotten hay, what looks like old leather saddles. There are no rules as to what to burn, we learned that from Annonay. I'm relieved it's been taken on board.

From the courtyard come cheers, applause, the roar

of voices. Excited, I nudge Pierre; he nudges back and grins. Moments later, we see the reason for all the noise. It's the Montgolfiers. They're walking round from the courtyard to our side of the Palace, shoulders straight, chins up. They look different – braver, more determined, 'Like soldiers going to battle,' I murmur to Pierre. I can tell he's pleased by that idea.

The Montgolfiers stop by the fire. Shake their heads. Give orders. Pierre and I crane our necks to watch. Monsieur Joseph, in a blue and gold coat that fits too tightly, keeps checking a scrap of paper in his hand. In the end, he's had to make do without the notebooks. But then he never did much like writing notes and, as things have turned out, maybe it's better that way.

Monsieur Etienne, ever the showman, wanders round the entire balloon, hands behind his back like he's on an evening stroll. He stops every few paces to inspect some detail. Guards, servants, important-looking men all hover beside him, hanging on his every word. So do we. Not that we can hear what's said, but we're watching, holding our breath.

At last it seems he's happy.

A nod to Monsieur Joseph and more servants rush forward to attach the ropes. You can almost taste the tension in the air. And oh how I wish I was down there in the thick of it. Far easier that, than standing here doing nothing. My feet fidget endlessly. I smooth my frock, touch the brooch still pinned to the front of it. I wish everything would just hurry up.

Two servants then appear round the side of the Palace carrying an enormous wicker basket on their shoulders.

'What's that for?' Pierre asks.

'It's what they'll put the animals in, I expect,' I reply, which brings on another wave of nerves because each time we've tried to tie things to the bottom of the balloon, well, let's just say it hasn't gone to plan. Though I don't remind Pierre of this fact.

The passengers come next.

People stand back to let them through, clapping and cheering and waving flags. It's Lancelot I see first, as Ginger Moustache leads her towards the balloon. Muzzle held high, she carries herself like she's already famous. She's enjoying all the attention, I can tell.

Servants carrying crates follow behind. In one, I can just about see a dark orange shape, not moving. I feel a pang in my chest for Coco.

'Bon voyage, little prince,' I murmur.

The crate behind carries Voltaire. Something's not right, though. Coming from inside is an awful screechy sound. I've never heard him make a noise like it before. Even up on the rooftop I can hear it. Pierre does too. He goes very tense and very quiet.

'He'll be all right in a minute,' I say quickly. 'It's probably just the noise of the crowd.'

But we both know Voltaire is a brave, proud duck. It's Coco who'll be scared, not him.

Pierre steps unsteadily out onto the roof.

'Come and sit down,' I say, patting the place beside me again because he's making me nervous.

'Voltaire's terrified. Listen to him. I can't leave him!' Pierre cries. He's proper upset, flinging his arms about, which only makes him wobble more.

'All right,' I say, trying to stay calm. 'We'll . . . we'll . . . Just don't do anything stupid!'

Yet the words are barely out of my mouth before he's swinging his legs over the edge of the roof.

25

One second he's there. The next, he's gone. I'm stuck to the spot, horrified. All I can see in my mind's eye is the gruesome, pulpy mess Pierre'll make when he hits the courtyard below. Yet I'm aware that no one's screaming down there, so eventually, I tell myself to be brave and risk a look.

Deep in the crowd I see the top of Pierre's curly head. My legs go weak with relief. He's upright and moving, pushing against the hordes, though he's not making much progress. Voltaire's crate is still a few hundred yards away: inside it, the dreadful screeching goes on.

I need to get down there. An extra pair of elbows to dig through the crowds. Together we might reach Voltaire in time to soothe him or save him. Whatever it takes to stop that horrible noise. To my right there's a hefty gutter pipe, perfect for shinning down, which I'm guessing was Pierre's way off the roof. Dreaming of breeches, I tuck up my blasted skirts and follow suit.

It's like jumping into a fast-flowing river. The second my feet touch the ground I'm swept along by the crowd. I'm carried almost back as far as the court-yard again. Forget elbows, it takes all my strength to stay standing, and by now I've lost sight of Pierre.

And still the people keep coming. Moving amongst the crowd are servants carrying platters of balloon-shaped biscuits. High above the rabble, on the Palace balconies, counts and countesses and other important types are gathering. The scene is all white wigs and fluttering fans – it's like staring up at an enormous dovecote.

On the central balcony is the King himself. Beside him is the Queen, wearing the most eye-popping outfit I've ever seen. Everything is bright blue and dazzling gold – *real* gold by the looks of it, just like the brooch I'm wearing. The Queen's skirts alone are wide enough to fill the entire balcony, and as for her wig – *alors*, her wig! – well, it towers above her head like a thundercloud. Attached to it is what looks like a toy version of the blue and gold balloon. Gabrielle is with her, talking, laughing and wearing a smaller version of the same wig, and even that's so tall it quivers when she turns her head.

It's the height of fashion, I bet people are saying, though when I think of how the Queen bargained with the King for her outfit, I'd rather have Lancelot any day of the week.

A stroke of luck and the crowd-tide begins to turn. People are moving closer to the fire now, and using all my strength, I'm able to fight my way towards the front.

Only ten, maybe twenty yards ahead is the balloon itself. It's no longer flat on the ground, but is starting to float, to plump up with air. Above people's heads, through gaps in the crowd, I glimpse gold leaves, bows, swirls. It's so magnificent I feel a great smile spread across my face. The magic has begun.

Everything this close to the balloon is now a whirl of action. Shouting. Pushing. Heat from the fire. Guards are ordering people to stand back. Somewhere in amongst it all, Voltaire is still complaining. And then Monsieur Etienne's voice: 'What the deuce is the matter with that duck?'

Perhaps it's because everyone's forced to move back that I spot a sudden opening in the crowd. Elbows out, I push through. People push back, shout, try to grab or slap me.

When I come up for air there is none, only heat, so

hot it scorches through my frock. I'm right in front of the fire now yet still can't see Pierre anywhere. It's all guards, servants, people rushing around doing last-minute checks. And Monsieur Etienne. When he spots me he's furious.

'What on EARTH? You can't just turn up here!' he yells.

'But Pierre . . .' I stutter. 'It's Voltaire . . .'

He keeps shouting: 'We're not playing at this anymore, Magpie! This isn't a little experiment in the orchard!'

'If it wasn't for our "little experiment",' I spit back, 'We wouldn't be here today!'

Before we can say more Monsieur Joseph appears and hands me a rope. He's angry too, I can tell, but his is the frosty, silent kind.

'I don't want to hear your excuses,' he says. 'Just hold this rope and do exactly as I say for once!'

I nod. I want to help, I really do. But I'm worried about Pierre, and stuck here holding a rope I'm not sure I'll find him.

As the Versailles clock chimes the hour, a cannon booms, so loud I feel it through my feet. The crowd go 'ahhh' in excitement. On the count of three, the fabric is nudged further into the air. The ropes go taut. Above our heads, the balloon keeps growing. It's so huge now it's almost blocking out the sky. More fuel is added to the fire. Another wave of heat hits me. Take-off, I know, is only minutes away.

'Steadyyyy with the ropes,' Monsieur Etienne cries, like he's soothing a nervous horse.

There's another great 'ooooooohhhhh!' from the crowd, as above our heads, the balloon grows taller and fatter. Slowly, almost lazily, it rights itself until it's in position for take-off. All that's left to do now is to attach the passenger basket. This time, it takes more than two servants to carry it. I'm guessing the passengers are already on board.

'Mind your backs!' one of the servants cries, as we step aside to let them through.

As the basket passes close by, I smell sheep fleece. Voltaire's fussy quack comes from inside. Shame Pierre didn't reach him in time, though thankfully he sounds calmer now, more his usual self. I hear Coco too, making his oh-so-familiar clucking sound like someone clearing their throat. I want to touch the basket, wish him luck. But both hands are full of rope. And as Monsieur Etienne roars: 'Stand back for the signal!' the basket passes on by to be tied to the balloon.

My arms are really starting to ache. More shouting. More people running and pulling. Everything's happening so fast. The cannon booms a second time: the take-off signal.

'Time to loosen the ropes!' Monsieur Etienne yells. 'Slowly now!'

We let them out a few inches at first. Then a few feet. What were great heaps of rope on the ground quickly unravel. As the pull of the balloon gets stronger, it's all we can do to keep hold at all.

Suddenly, there's another commotion at the front of the crowd. A woman has pushed her way through. She's shouting and waving her arms about. A cold feeling trickles down the back of my neck when I see how she really *does* stand out like a crow.

'Stop the flight!' Madame Delacroix yells. 'I demand it! Stop at once!'

She's too late. The flight's about to happen and there's nothing she can do. Then, she sees me. She stops shouting and stares instead, a look that strips the skin from my bones.

'You little *thief*!' Madame Delacroix spits at me.

It's hardly an insult. Yet she's so poisonous with it, I'm afraid. Her sights are fixed beyond me though: she's moving in on the Montgolfiers. Monsieur Etienne, frowning, backs away. Monsieur Joseph is completely bewildered.

'Listen to me, Etienne. And you, Joseph,' she says. 'Do as I say and you'll have your notebooks back. I'll walk away and you can carry on as if nothing has happened.'

I lick my lips. She's holding something and adjusts her grip. Her hands must be hot inside those gloves when we're this close to the fire.

Monsieur Etienne lunges for her. In the tail of my eye, I see a flash of silver.

'Watch out!' Monsieur Joseph cries. 'She's got a sword!'

She swings the blade high above her head, then down again. Air rushes past my ear. Before I know what is happening, something cold and sharp presses against my neck.

26

'Stand back!' Madame Delacroix snarls like a hunting dog with a dead rabbit it won't give up. 'Don't any of you come near!'

She's got me: arm round my shoulders, sword at my throat. I can't move a muscle. And I'm still holding this blasted balloon rope. The ache in my arms is fast becoming unbearable. I'm not sure how much longer I can hang on.

Monsieur Etienne tries again to grab the weapon from her.

'I'm warning you,' she says, swinging the sword in his direction this time. 'I'll use this if I have to.'

Now I see it properly it's a scary great thing – a good few feet of silver. She must've swiped it from a careless guard. Monsieur Etienne holds up his hands in defeat. 'Stop this, Camille. I don't know what you want, but this isn't the way to go about it.'

Camille. Etienne. First names. They *know* each other?

I'm properly confused. Hadn't she been working for the enemy? Didn't she want those papers to sell on so that an English inventor could claim his flying machine was the first?

I'd assumed this was a simple case of fame and money – lots of both, the sort of amounts people went crazy over.

First names, though, makes it personal. Madame Delacroix – Camille – doesn't waste time in saying so, either.

'You're lucky,' she goes on. 'To have an invention that'll put your name in the history books. You'll be the toast of France, won't you?'

'Not if we don't get on with it,' Monsieur Etienne points out.

The crowd nearest to us can see what's happening. They're stunned, silent. But, further back, people are getting restless. Someone shouts, 'Come on! What're we waiting for?' There's a cheer of agreement.

'Put the weapon down,' Monsieur Joseph pleads. He's sweating like a pig. 'Whatever it is you want, we can talk. But not now; the King's waiting.'

I can hardly feel my arms anymore. The other

people holding on to the ropes are complaining too. But Camille isn't going to rush.

'All my life I've lived in your shadows,' she says, 'You had the attention, the education, the opportunities to achieve great things. What did I have?'

Monsieur Etienne interrupts: 'Camille, stop—'

'What I had,' she keeps talking, her voice high and tight, 'Was a mother's love. She promised me magic. And in the end, when you already had so much, you took that away from me too.'

She's ranting. She must be mad. But when I glance at the Montgolfiers they're both looking so shifty I'm suddenly not sure. The point of the sword is back against my throat again, pressing ever harder. She's sweating too – we all are – as the flames get higher and brighter.

I can't hold my rope any more.

As I let go, the balloon lurches upwards – only in one corner though, throwing the whole thing off balance.

'Watch out! It's coming down!' someone wails. And suddenly everyone's rushing and shouting again. The crowd pushes against us, against Camille. Taken by surprise her sword slips – at least I think it does. I feel it scrape down my throat, before the panic kicks in.

'Get off me!' I scream.

But she's still pinching my arm, and her face, close to mine, is tight with hate.

'Once a thief, always a thief!' she hisses. 'But not any more. I want my brooch back.'

Her spit's on my cheeks. I try to spit back. Bite. Anything to get away. Then I feel a sharp tugging at the front of my frock. The fabric tears. And just like that she lets go of me so fast it propels me backwards.

I fall against the passenger basket. It's bumping along the ground, dangerously close to the fire. From inside, I hear bleating and clucking. Those poor animals! I have to get them out before the whole thing crashes into the flames.

I've already hooked my arms over the rim, when Monsieur Etienne yells for me to keep away.

I ignore him. With a kick, I get one leg over the side. No one else can hold onto their ropes. One by one in quick succession, as they let go, the basket begins to lift.

For a very long moment, I'm stuck. Half in, half out. My heart's in my throat. Just when I start slipping to the ground, a hand grabs my frock. A great heave and I'm pulled properly inside the basket.

'What the—?' I yelp.

With a great thud, I land at Lancelot's feet. She's tied to the side of the basket, eating a pile of grass. I see the two bird crates, Coco and Voltaire still inside.

Sat with his fingers curled round the bars of one of them is Pierre, who looks about to be sick.

'Honestly, Magpie, it was the only way I could get Voltaire to calm down,' he tries explaining.

As I crawl across the floor to sit next to him, I make light of it. 'Fancy seeing you here. Thought you didn't like flying.'

'I don't,' he replies. 'And your moving about's making it worse.'

Poor Pierre. He's done this for Voltaire and my chest aches for him. If I could get them both back down safely, I honestly would. But the tethering ropes hang slack against the balloon. It's too late to stop the flight. We're floating free.

I sit tight until the rocking slows. Then I reach for Pierre's hand. It feels cold and clammy, like it had that day when he'd wound the rope too tight around his wrist and got dragged into the sky. This time's different. We're inside a basket, together, with a balloon full of hot air above us. What's more, the King of France is watching. The horror of the last few minutes slides away. I start smiling: I can't help myself.

'You might not believe me,' I tell Pierre. 'But you're going to enjoy this.'

'Don't be stupid, Magpie. I'm going to throw up.' Which he does over the side in spectacular fashion.

When he's finally finished, I open the bird crates. It

is wonderful to see Coco again, and he nestles in the crook of my arm like nothing is amiss. Lancelot too, legs splayed for balance, nuzzles my foot like she remembers me at last and breathes gently on Coco. Even Voltaire looks his usual dignified self again.

'Don't know what you had to panic about,' I tell him. 'You're the only one of us who can actually fly. If this balloon goes down, you'll be fine.'

'Shut up!' Pierre wails. He's got his eyes closed. If only he'd open them and look up, he'd see.

Above our heads, the balloon has swelled magnificently. Against its bright blue and gold, even the sky seems a little faded. It must look brilliant from the ground. Not that I'd want to be down there: this is the very best place to be, especially as we're still gaining height.

The noise of the crowd grows fainter as we drift away from the Palace. It's so peaceful. Soon, all I can hear is the sighing of the balloon, and next to me, Lancelot chomping grass. Coco's snoring, Voltaire's perched on Pierre's lap. We could almost be at home in the orchard, all together under a tree, *that's* how calm it feels.

My mind drifts back to the very start, all those months ago in that field, or rather, in the sky above it. The world had, in that moment, looked so different. It made me think that things could change if only you saw them differently.

Very slowly, I get to my feet.

Pierre's eyes ping open straight away. 'Don't move! Stay still!'

'It's not going to tip up,' I reassure him.

Keeping my hands on the basket rim, I peer out for the very first time.

'Oh, my!' I breathe. 'This is *incredible*!'

We're over the gardens that surround Versailles. Behind us, the Palace is as small as a pile of toy bricks. At the front of it is the courtyard, packed with tiny dots. Beyond, paths and driveways span out like spokes from a wheel. Everything is cream-coloured or green, every line part of a pattern. No wonder the Queen's farm was so perfect – the whole *world* looks that way from up here.

'Pierre, you really should see this.'

He shakes his head. 'I can't.'

I feel my stomach lifting. We're going higher. Suddenly though, Pierre leaps to his feet like he's been stung by wasps.

'The filthy beast has just . . . ugh!' His breeches are splattered brown, and stinking to high heaven. 'It's eaten so much grass it's got the flux!'

Lancelot, noble as ever, keeps chewing.

'Stand here, beside me, and hold on to the edge,' I tell him, trying not to laugh. I don't tell him he smells worse than old cabbage. I'm just glad he's got his eyes open at last.

As well as drifting up, we're moving away from the Palace gardens now. There are more trees, acres of parkland with lakes sunk into the ground.

'*Oh*, Magpie!' Pierre gasps. '*C'est merveilleux!*'

'Isn't it fantastic?'

He nods shakily. 'I didn't know the world could look like this. Oh, everyone should see it! Everyone should get the chance to fly, shouldn't they?'

'Yes, they should,' I agree, glancing at him sideways, 'Even people who thought they'd be scared.'

A wide smile spreads across his face. Seeing him like that makes me smile too, though the best part of everything is having my favourite person in all the world here to share it with me.

'Magpie.' Pierre turns serious. 'You do realize we're the very first people in history to fly in a balloon, don't you?'

He's right. No other living creature has been up in the air before. Even the animals here with us are the first to try a flight like this, to see how they fared. We've beaten the English, Madame Delacroix, a couple of robbery attempts. We've even beaten the Montgolfiers themselves, who've made a balloon but never set foot in one.

'We're not *supposed* to be up here though, are we?'

I remind him. 'So it might not count, you know, in the history books and all that.'

'*We* know, though, don't we Magpie?' Pierre says.

I nod: we do. No history book can take that from us. I'm so lost in it all, I don't notice that Pierre's staring at me. It's a funny, wide-eyed expression he's got. I just hope he's not about to ruin the moment by going moony on me or something.

'What's up with *you*?' I ask, a bit sharp.

He points to the front of my frock. 'The brooch. It's gone.'

'I think that crazy lady with the sword took it,' I say.

Looking down, I see a tear in the fabric just below my collarbone where the brooch had been. In its place is a big, dark stain.

Pierre's suddenly looking sick again. 'You've been hurt.'

The stain is wet. I frown, touch it, taste it.

It's blood.

27

It probably looks worse than it is. If it was really bad, it'd be painful, wouldn't it, and all I can feel is a little bit of stinging in my chest. There's a stupid amount of blood, though. It's all over my hands. As I go to wipe them in the skirt of my frock, I find that's bloody too, which is annoying. I want to be gazing at the view not tending to a stupid scratch.

With something to focus on, Pierre stops looking green about the gills and becomes quite bossy. He tears an arm off his shirt and folds it into a sort of pad.

'Press it hard against your chest,' he instructs me. 'And keep it there. It'll stop the bleeding.'

I do as he says, though it hurts then – a nasty, leg-buckling pain. I don't mention it, mind you. I just want to get back to enjoying the ride.

Beneath us is a long, thin ribbon of dirt, which I guess is the main road back to Paris. Every so often, we pass over a house, a barn. In one field, a group of horses sets off galloping and bucking at the sight of us. There are birds who shriek, people on the ground who wave. It's incredible. I want to stay up here for ever.

'You all right?' Pierre asks more than once. 'You look cold.'

'I'm great!' I tell him, though I do feel a bit light-headed.

When the basket gives its first little shudder I hardly notice. The second time, it's more of a shake – and quite a strong one. Glancing up, I notice the balloon is rippling as if it's lost air.

It's Pierre who spots the tear. It's a third of the way up the balloon, curved, about a yard in length. It looks newly done, jagged round the edges, like someone's taken a swipe at it with a sharp weapon. The dread hits me when I realize I'm not the only thing Camille Delacroix has cut.

'It's not that big,' I say, trying to stay upbeat.

'You said that about your wound,' Pierre points out.

And really, I know any tear isn't good – in a person *or* a balloon. A cold sweat breaks out on my forehead. Our flight is going to be over sooner than we thought.

With a jolt, we begin to lose height quite quickly. Coco chooses this moment to wake up so I put him down on the floor. Lancelot, finally realizing she isn't in a field, starts pacing, which makes the basket rock, and Voltaire flap his wings in panic. Pierre braces himself against the basket. He looks as pale as I feel.

We're dropping fast. And it seems to be getting faster. Beneath us the treetops loom closer. I see details again – the colour of curtains at a window, the swishing of a horse's tail. Above us, the balloon topples to the side. Instead of drifting straight down, we seem to be at an angle. Just up ahead is another road – this one's a crossroads. There's plenty of traffic on it: horses, carriages, people on foot, all staring up at us. I pray we don't come down on top of them.

'Will there be a bump when we land?' Pierre asks.

'A little one,' I lie.

Somehow, the balloon limps on for a few hundred more yards. We brush the tops of a copse of trees. Then, before us a blessed sight: open ground. Standing in the middle is a person who, as we close in, I see is a boy with fair hair. My heart goes double time because it's Sebastien.

'Oi! Watch out!' I yell. 'We're going to land! Grab a rope if you can!'

Coming in low, we're on course to clip Sebastien's right shoulder. Just in time he goes sideways and we avoid him. Then we hit the ground once. Twice. The basket tips over. There's a scratching of claws, flapping wings, beaks, hooves and Pierre and me all tangled up together. Everything's spinning. With a final thump, it stops.

What comes next is a very long silence. I feel a mad throbbing sensation in my chest. My frock is wet, sticking to my skin. I don't need to look to know it's blood. Someone starts groaning; I think it's Pierre. Out on the field, Lancelot is already grazing. Voltaire rushes from the basket then stops to paddle his feet in the grass. If a duck could ever look glad to be on firm ground, he does. Yet a few yards away, Coco lies still.

As soon as I move, the pain spikes under my ribs. I catch my breath as the field spins. Somehow, I drag myself the short distance to Coco. I'm hoping, *begging* he's just stunned.

'Come on little friend,' I murmur, scooping him into my arms. 'Time to wake up.'

I stroke his chest in tiny circles, just the way he likes it. Finally, he opens one eye, then the other. I'm so relieved I want to cry.

Then, the biggest surprise.

Coco, my silent, sleepy rooster, tips back his head and crows. And crows some more, on and on, and so loud they probably hear it in England.

I'm still laughing with relief when a hand touches

my shoulder. I look up to see Sebastien standing beside me, staring at the wrecked balloon in absolute amazement. Well, I suppose it *is* amazing to see two people and three animals drop from the sky. Maybe it's shock, or the surprise of seeing him again, but my teeth start chattering and I come over all shivery-cold.

Pierre, wiping his hand on his breeches, offers it to Sebastien, who shakes it.

'About the duel—' Pierre starts to say. But Sebastien's noticed I'm shaking and tries to put an arm round my shoulders. The pain makes me yelp.

'Oh!' He pulls away. I've left blood all down the side of his shirt. Quite a lot of it too.

'It's just a scratch. Don't fuss,' I tell him.

Yet the sight of all that red makes my head spin, and before I know it, I'm lying flat out on the grass. Sebastien crouches beside me, his lovely face knotted with concern. 'It's more than a scratch, Magpie. You need a surgeon, *tout de suite!*'

'I suppose you're going to offer to help me again, are you?' I say, looking him straight in the eye.

He laughs easily. 'That's not a *challenge to my honour,* is it?'

It's meant in jest, I know. But there's something about him today. Don't know what. Until I see his hand, that is, the same hand he was flexing yesterday, which despite him denying it, is swollen and bruised. I can't think why he'd lie.

Between them, Pierre and Sebastien manage to prop me up. But by the time an open carriage and horses comes thundering across the field in our direction, I'm flagging badly. It's Monsieur Joseph who jumps out first, and rushes to us. Monsieur Etienne makes a beeline for the balloon.

'Idiot boy!' Monsieur Joseph cries, crushing Pierre in a hug. I wonder if this is the telling off he's been fearing: if it is then we've not much to worry about.

Next, a man I've never seen before appears. 'I'm Monsieur de Rozier,' he says. 'I've an interest in science and am here to check the animals survived the flight.'

'*Animals?*' Pierre cries. 'What about Magpie?'

'I might've known you'd be in this together!' Monsieur Joseph remarks. 'What possessed you to do something so dangerous?'

'Poultry, mostly,' I admit.

He splutters, almost smiles. Then sees the blood and cries out.

'Bandages, quickly!' he snaps his fingers at Monsieur de Rozier. 'And water and brandy! Hurry!'

As Monsieur de Rozier rushes back to the carriage, I glimpse another passenger still inside: a dark dress, sleek black hair. That old feeling of dread comes over me again.

'She came quietly in the end,' Monsieur Joseph remarks, following my gaze. 'I think we've all got some explaining to do when we get back to the palace.'

Madame Delacroix – *Camille* – sits alone in the carriage, her hands in her lap like they've been tied together. Even now, she's still wearing her gloves. I look away. I'm tired of her – tired of even trying to keep my eyes open.

I don't shut them, though. And I wish I had. When everyone's talking and fussing over me and he thinks no one's watching, Sebastien goes over to the carriage. One foot on the step, he starts talking to Camille. I can't hear what's being said at first. Not until I catch a few words of it and realize with a shudder: they're talking in English.

So much for honour.

It's as if we're back in the air, gazing down on familiar things that, from high up, look very different. Except I'm not flying any more. I'm in the middle of a field watching the handsome boy who'd wanted to help me deep in conversation with the one person who for months now, most definitely did not.

'They *know* each other?' Pierre's shocked too.

I nod dismally. 'Seems that way.'

What Sebastien's part in all this is, I don't properly know. I just feel such a fool – I'm usually smarter than this, but with him I let down my guard. I reckon I was closest to knowing the truth about him back in that Paris street when he'd offered to carry the box. The whole thing makes me feel exhausted.

Monsieur de Rozier returns with his bandages and brandy. He tries to move me but the pain makes me almost faint.

'We need to get her to the surgeon at the palace,' he says, shaking his head. 'She's losing too much blood.'

At least I *think* that's what he says. He sounds really far away all of a sudden, like he's underwater. Everything's gone twilight-dark. I feel strange. But Pierre's still here with me, and Coco's tucked under my arm, so I'm not alone.

And we *flew*, I think, a warm, peaceful feeling spreading through me. Whatever happens now, at least we flew.

28

It turns out I'm a fighter. That's what the surgeon says after he's sewn up a three-inch hole in my chest. He makes me bite down on a leather strap for the pain. It doesn't help, but at least I don't faint again.

'She's tough, this one,' Monsieur Etienne agrees; he sounds impressed. 'I knew it from the moment I saw her.'

It also turns out that Pierre and his shirt sleeve saved my life. Without his quick action to slow the bleeding I'd probably not have made it.

'You did the same for me once, remember?' Pierre says when I try to thank him. 'And back then you didn't even know who I was.'

Oh yes I did, I think guiltily, *I really did*. But we settle on a teary '*Merci*', and leave it there.

I'm moved from the surgeon's table to a huge white bed and given more brandy and strict orders to rest. Tired and sore though I am, I want news. And Coco. I beg Pierre for both, so when the maid tending me isn't looking, he sneaks Coco in under a blanket. But as for news of the balloon and the King's reaction, he shakes his head: 'Papa wants to speak to us about it.'

So I guess the telling off is still to come, after all.

It's dark when I wake up. It must be the same day – even though the windows are closed, I can still hear the crowd outside. Someone's lit the candles, and sitting next to my bed is Monsieur Joseph. Monsieur Etienne is with him, arms folded. From the other side of the bed, I hear quacking, so I know Pierre and Voltaire are here too. It feels daft to be just lying here, so helpless. Though when I try to wriggle up the bed, I'm too weak.

'You're angry, aren't you?' I say warily.

'*Angry?*' Monsieur Etienne's eyebrows go sky-high. 'My dear child, what you did put the whole flight in jeopardy! It took some pretty fast talking, let me tell you, to persuade the King you'd not been planted in that balloon basket by the English!'

I pluck at the bedsheet, ashamed. Beside me Pierre swallows noisily. Now, in the light of day, I can see how stupid we've been. I mean, we'd been arrested as spies, hadn't we, so of course it looked suspicious. What makes it worse is that I start to cry.

'We didn't mean it,' I sob. 'Pierre was worried about Voltaire, and I got hurt by Madame—'

'Stop, Magpie, that's enough.' Monsieur Joseph puts his hand over mine. 'Now, listen to me, both of you. What you did today was very dangerous and I'm furious with you.'

Except, oddly, he doesn't sound it. Looking up, I see he's trying to keep a straight face. Monsieur Etienne doesn't even bother to hide it, he's now beaming from ear to ear. My mouth falls open. I laugh, unsure, then glance at Pierre, who's smiling too.

'It's all right,' he says.

And it is.

Maybe because I feel safe at last, amongst friends, I start to cry a bit more. Me and Pierre have done something no one else in the whole world has done. Together, we've flown in a balloon. Of course it was reckless. We didn't know if it would fly or be safe, or if we'd come back to earth in one piece. But I've never been good at following rules.

'Magpie,' Monsieur Joseph says. 'Oh Magpie.' And the way he says it, warmed with a smile, makes it probably the nicest thing anyone's ever said to me. There's a bit of awkward shuffling. An 'ouch' from me as he tries to wrap his arms round my shoulders, but in the end he settles for planting a kiss on the top of my head.

When he pulls away Monsieur Joseph takes out notebook and pencil.

'I must have your account of the flight,' he says to Pierre and me. 'Tonight, before you forget it.'

'I'll never forget it,' I assure him.

Once I've been revived with hot chocolate and a meat pie, it's pretty exhilarating to go over the whole experience again: every sight, every sound, every movement – even Lancelot's upset stomach. As we speak, Monsieur Joseph makes notes – lots and lots of notes – and Monsieur Etienne questions us until my head begins to droop.

Eventually, Monsieur Joseph lays down his pencil. 'We've achieved great things here today, everyone. To make that balloon fly was the work of many months and many people. There were times when we thought it could never succeed. Yet, despite what fate chose to throw at us, today was a resounding success.'

Fate.

The wound in my chest starts throbbing.

'Did you get the brooch back from Camille?' I ask.

Monsieur Joseph rubs a hand over his face. Glances at Monsieur Etienne, who goes to a side table and pours himself a glass of water.

'It's a bit more complicated than that, Magpie,' Monsieur Etienne says. I get the sense he doesn't want to talk about it, which makes me push.

'How? She stole it. You were there. You saw her do it.' I don't mention what she called me, but I've a nasty feeling they might've heard that too.

'As far as we're aware she's still got the brooch,' Monsieur Joseph says wearily.

I'm surprised. I look at Pierre, who's frowning.

'But it was expensive, wasn't it?' he asks.

Monsieur Joseph shrugs.

'And what about the notebooks in the box?' Now I'm confused. 'You know a man came for them, don't you? He's a spy for the English — a proper one, I mean. It's him who smashed up Pierre's face.'

Monsieur Joseph flinches at this, but shakes his head. 'No, Delamere's not a spy.'

'They caught him,' I argue, surprised Monsieur Joseph knows his name too. 'He's down in the cellar with all the others.'

It's Monsieur Etienne who comes over and sits at the foot of my bed.

'Magpie,' he says, so gently it makes me nervous. 'This is to go no further, but I think the King got rather carried away on security matters these past few days. I don't actually believe *any* of those poor people he rounded up are English spies.'

Pierre gasps. 'What, *none* of them?'

I'm starting to feel dizzy again. None of it makes sense. This has always been about the notebooks. Always. Right from the break-in on that very first night.

'So Madame Delacroix isn't a spy?' I say, to be clear. 'Camille isn't working for the English?'

'No. Nor's her husband, Monsieur Delamere.'

My hunch was right then! They were working together.

'How do you know her, anyway?' I ask.

A glance passes between the Montgolfiers.

'By birth,' Monsieur Joseph says. 'She's our sister.'

I stare at him. He's not lying. Or smiling. He means it. Of course he does. It's why they know each other's first names.

Camille Delacroix is a Montgolfier.

I shut my eyes; I have to, to stop the room spinning. I wonder if I'm still in shock from all that blood, or whether it's because there's something here I've misunderstood.

'She didn't *steal* the brooch, not exactly,' Monsieur Joseph says. 'It was hers in the first place. It's always been hers. How it came to be hidden in that box I don't know.'

The box was what she wanted, what she sent me into the house that night to fetch. Not papers, not notebooks: the box. Because all the time that gold brooch was tucked away in the lining.

There's a creak in the bed as Monsieur Etienne stands up. 'Let's talk about it in the morning, shall we? You're exhausted.'

I open my eyes. Monsieur Joseph is on his feet now too. Pierre's carrying Voltaire under his arm. They're all leaving.

'Don't go!' I'm desperate for them to stay and tell me Camille's story because there must be one – no one's that angry without reason.

Monsieur Joseph mistakes my interest for fear.

'Don't worry, you're safe tucked away up here,' he says. 'Camille won't hurt you again. She's spending the night down in the cells. They're taking her to the city jail in the morning. From there we'll determine if she's a criminal or just very sick.'

It's amazing how cool he sounds about his own sister. Not that I've forgotten how she threatened me – *attacked* me – so I suppose it's justice of sorts. Yet something about all this still makes me uneasy. I can't put my finger on it. But I think people are made of good *and* bad, and that nobody, not even thieves or English spies or scorned sisters, are all one or the other. I'd say that applies to Sebastien too.

If I want to hear Camille's side of the story I'd better ask her myself, tonight, while I've still got the chance.

29

It's a stupid idea; I realize it as soon as I get out of
bed. Somehow, I make it across the room and down
the hallway, stopping when the pain gets too much.
The stairs are easier, I just cling to the bannister. Once
I'm downstairs there's no going back.

The guard on duty by the prison hatch is Ginger
Moustache. Word must've got round that I'm not a
spy because he greets me like an old pal.

'Call me Monsieur Cedric,' he says.

'Magpie.' We shake hands.

'Can't think why you want to talk to her,'
Monsieur Cedric says, when I tell him why I'm here.
'Nasty piece, if you ask me.'

But he helps me through the little door and leads
the way with a lamp. At the top of the steps, I hesitate,

my heart thump-thumping. I still don't like cellars.

'You all right?' Monsieur Cedric asks.

I take a deep breath. I've flown in a balloon and survived a sword attack; yes, I am all right.

Camille's wide awake in her cell. Though she keeps her distance, I'm still glad of the prison bars between us. I ask Monsieur Cedric for something to sit on. He brings me an old wine crate which I sink down onto, gladly, my legs feeling like chewed string.

'Comfy enough, are you?' Camille says.

Though I can't quite see her face, I'm nervous.

'I want to ask you something,' I say.

She shrugs. 'Ask away. Doesn't mean I'll tell you.'

'Why did you want the brooch so badly?'

Camille narrows her eyes at me. Thinking. Deciding what to say. It's prickly, being stared at like that. Makes me want to scratch myself all over.

'It's mine,' she says. 'My mother wanted me to have it when she died.'

'So why was it hidden in Monsieur Joseph's valuables box?'

'Everything in our family goes to the men, right down to the paintings on the walls and the carpets on the floors.'

'The Montgolfiers told me you're related,' I say. The idea of them being family is going to take some getting used to, though it explains why she knew the inside of the house so well.

She comes towards me now, so at last I see her properly. She's wearing the gold brooch at the neck of her dress, and all over again I'm struck by how beautiful it is.

'Do you have a family, Magpie?' she asks.

'No,' I admit. These days, more and more, my parents seem as faint to me as shadows. 'It's just me and Coco.'

'You're lucky,' she says. 'An unhappy family is worse than no family.'

'But you must've grown up in Annonay in that nice house,' I point out. 'And, all right, so Monsieur Etienne's a bit sure of himself, but Monsieur Joseph is kind and—'

She raises her hand. Those gloves are looking proper tatty. 'Enough about my brothers. It's my father you need to hear about – the great paper manufacturer of Annonay.'

I nod. I know about the family paper factory.

'Everyone used to say what a fine man he was – good to his workers. Fair. But what they didn't know was at home, with us, he was a tyrant. Do you know what that means?'

'He was mean?' I offer.

'Exactly that. The worst thing was I wasn't allowed

260

to think. Being a girl, I stood by while he forced my brothers to learn, bullying them through lessons I could've picked up in an instant if I'd been given the chance.'

I can picture it, she's sharp, all right: blade-sharp. Next to her, the Montgolfiers seem slower, rounder at the edges. They're a darned sight kinder, too.

'So I took it upon myself to learn.' She pauses, flexing her fingers on the bars. 'I liked building things, making equipment and solving problems – exactly the sort of knowledge my father thought a girl shouldn't have.'

Funny, but I know what she means because that's how my brain works too.

'I started working on a special machine in secret. It was meant for cutting paper. Father was always complaining how they didn't have a decent blade at the factory, so I wanted to surprise him. To show him what I was capable of.'

'And did you?' I ask. Already, I've got a bad feeling about this story of hers.

'It was his birthday,' she says. 'As the machine was ready and working, I gave it to him as a present. Everyone else had made him stupid little cards, but I'd created something original and clever. And do you know what he did when he saw it?'

I shake my head.

'He ordered the servants to take it away. Then, in front of everyone, he told me I was an embarrassment to him and my brothers. I must be ill, he said, to think I could invent something when I'd had no education, and if that was the case then I should go to my room straight away.'

'Did you?'

'Yes. I stayed there for three whole months,' she says with a defiant lift of the chin.

I don't suppose for a second she spent the time crying in bed, either. What she says next confirms it.

'If anything, my father's reaction spurred me on. Whilst he thought I was in my room resting, I was busy designing – a bigger, better cutting machine, and not one for paper either. This machine would bring me the recognition I *deserved*. In a few months it was ready. What I needed now was something to practise on. To cut. Something different.'

She keeps talking like she's getting into her stride. But the words 'cutting machine' snag on me. I need her to explain.

'What sort of "something to cut"?' I ask.

'A neck, I thought.'

I'm glad I'm sat down.

'I tried to borrow a hen—'

'*Borrow?*'

She ignores the interruption. 'But my sneaky

brothers caught me and threatened to tell our father, which is all rather rich, isn't it, considering they used *three* animals in their flying experiment today?'

I'm glad they did, frankly. It saved Coco and Voltaire from the pot. Not that I expect Camille to understand.

'In the end, I had to make do with a watermelon. But it went wrong. Horribly wrong.' And she lets go of the bars, pulls off her stained old gloves and there I see it. On her right hand, the two middle fingers are missing. The stumps are smooth and scarred. On the left, the thumb is crooked, like it broke and never mended.

'Oh!' I cover my mouth in shock.

'I was holding the melon to stop it rolling off the table. The blade dropped too soon, on to my hands and . . .' She mimes the horrible chopping action.

I wince.

She looks strangely pleased. 'Father said I deserved all I got.'

I stare at her mangled hands. I hate this woman. I'm scared of her. But right now, I also feel sorry for her. Even me, who's never known a father's love, can't believe he'd say such a thing to his own daughter.

'Did your father send you back to your room again?' I ask.

'I didn't give him the chance,' she replies, tugging the gloves back on with some difficulty. 'I was sixteen by then, so I ran away. I got my revenge in the way I knew best.'

'Which was?'

'To marry the enemy – an Englishman. Real name Delamere. We changed it to make it sound more French.'

'To Delacroix,' I say out loud.

I'd not noticed before but there's definitely a Montgolfier look to Camille – the way she kinks her eyebrows is just like Monsieur Etienne. All this time. All those years. The bitterness eating away at her like blowfly in a horse's neck.

My gaze slides back to the brooch, glinting in the half-light. 'What's the brooch got to do with all this?' I ask, because I'm still not sure.

'You've heard of Monsieur Guillotin, I take it?'

I have. He's the man behind the gruesome head-cutting-off machine that's in all the news-sheets and that I, in a darker moment yesterday, feared we were being lined up for.

She taps her chest. 'My idea. *My* cutting machine. I invented it first, though who'd believe a woman, eh?'

No one. The awful thing is, she's right.

But the *guillotine*!

With a shudder, I think of all the cartoons of sharp blades and blood and heads collected in baskets. What a dreadful thing to put your name to. Though of course if she'd had her way it would've been the 'Delacroix', or the 'Delamere'. Either way it's a killing machine. I can't imagine it: sitting down with note-book and pencil, sketching out designs, getting excited at the thought of it actually working.

No, I think, *my brain isn't like Camille's. Not at all.*

'My mother wasn't cruel like my father. She always told me I could do anything, that all I had to do was work hard and hope.' Camille touches the brooch. 'This was her favourite piece of jewellery. She'd tell me stories about how when she wore it, it made her feel as if she was floating on air. It was silly nonsense, really.'

Yet I'd felt something when I'd worn it, hadn't I? Like I was about to be lifted off my feet. 'It's not silly,' I blurt out, but she's not listening.

'Years later, when my mother died, my father refused to hand over the brooch. When I heard Guil-lotin had copied my idea, I became fixated on that brooch. It was like a talisman to me. If only I had it, I could do anything. I'd challenge Guillotin's patent, I'd make a name for myself. Like my mother promised, I'd be walking on air – do you see?'

I *do* see why she wanted me to steal back the brooch.

'But why did you pretend to want the papers?' I ask.

She smiles: nastily, spitefully. 'I wasn't *pretending*, Magpie. I simply wanted to scupper their chances. The more it looked like they'd succeed, the more I was set on ruining it for them, just like they'd done to me.'

It sinks in, bit by bit. She was never really interested in the papers themselves. They were just a reminder of what her brothers were achieving and all she'd lost.

'I won, though, didn't I, Magpie?' Camille says. 'It was all worth it in the end.'

'*Was* it?' I'm amazed to hear her say this.

It's no good me feeling sorry for her either, I realize. Though I've a clearer sense these days of what's right and what's definitely wrong, it's a line Camille Delacroix doesn't understand.

The pain's back in my chest. I'm weakening. It's time to end our talk. 'You got your brooch if that's what you mean,' I tell her. 'But you're the one in a prison cell, not your brothers. They're the toast of France.'

She stares at me. Like she might try to hit me, even with the prison bars between us. Then, her shoulders start to shake. Her head goes down. I sit forward, alarmed: is she *crying*?

No.

She looks up, her face all twisted. She's laughing.

Unsteadily, I get to my feet. I've had enough of

Camille Delacroix. I'm sorry for her horrible life, but being vengeful and bitter doesn't pay in the end. We succeeded today, and she failed. I look her straight in the eye, one last time, and I don't shrink at all.

As we head up the steps, Monsieur Cedric lets me lean on his arm. I need it.

'I feel a bit sorry for the son, to be honest,' he says. 'His mother blamed him for everything – threatened to kill him *and* his horse! If that's how the English treat their children, then I don't think much of them.'

I don't tell him that actually she's French. Nor do I let him see the tears in my eyes. Because any fool can guess who the son and horse are in this sorry story.

SEVEN

FOR A SECRET
NEVER TO BE TOLD

30

It should've brought us some sort of peace, and in a way it does. The flight is declared a spectacular triumph by the King and Queen of France, who celebrate with champagne and fireworks. The animals are given medals for bravery: Voltaire wears his round his neck, all proud, but every time I try to put Coco's on him he shakes his feathers and crows. Now he's found his voice he won't stop. Lancelot – sorry, Montauciel – goes down in history as the first ever flying sheep, though thankfully there's no record of what it did to her bowels. She returns to live a happy life on the Queen's farm. No one tells her that, in the Queen's eyes, she's second best to fashion. All that matters is she'll never be eaten, which for a sheep is decent enough.

Further afield, every news-sheet carries the story of the world's first flying machine, how it stayed in the air over Versailles for eight whole minutes, and only came down because of a tear in its side. Overnight, balloons become all the rage. Everyone's talking about them – which is funny really, when we worried about keeping it secret, though it makes a welcome change from guillotines. The Montgolfier design is copied onto dresses, wallpaper. The Queen keeps wearing tiny balloons in her wig. And the Montgolfiers' name – a French name, not an English one – is in the history books at last.

Life's looking up for me too. I've been welcomed into the Montgolfier family for good. Monsieur Joseph's even planning to make it official.

'As soon as we get back to Annonay I'll have adoption papers drawn up,' he tells me.

And so I start experiencing a sort of happiness I've never known before. It's not fluttery and giddy but steady and true, and every morning when I wake up it's still there. I've got a family name now too: Magpie Montgolfier which, I don't mind admitting, has a rather fine ring to it. Though I'm not so bothered about it being made official. I'm beginning to think we make too much fuss about papers.

When it's finally time to face the long journey home,

we set off early from Versailles, taking the main road as far as Paris before bearing south. The sun's only just up, the horses are fresh, the road is quiet. As it's too nice a morning to sit inside the carriage, Pierre and I are happily perched on the outside, swinging our legs from the back shelf. It's the best place for views and fresh air. Voltaire prefers it too; he's never been the same about small spaces after that crate. As for Coco, he just wants to crow. And crow. So we sit him on the roof and leave him to it.

A few miles west of Paris, I notice we're being followed. The lone rider is on a grey horse, and could easily overtake, but instead stays thirty or forty feet behind us.

'What's he up to?' I ask Pierre, who's noticed him too.

'Well, he can't be a robber. We've nothing worth stealing now, have we, Magpie?'

I glance sideways at Pierre, thinking it's an odd remark to make. But he says no more about it, and nor do I.

Just as we reach the outskirts of Paris, the rider finally pushes his horse into a gallop and speeds past. The road's dusty, busy. It happens so fast I almost miss it. A quick eyeful of the horse is all I need to be certain: it's Dante. The rider, crouched low over his horse's neck, looks like an ordinary boy enjoying a fast ride. And it makes me suddenly sad for the friendship that might've been.

'Hang on, isn't that—?' Pierre points as boy and horse whizz by.

I don't want to talk any more about Sebastien- it's still too confusing. All along he'd been working with his mother and father, and yet despite it I don't hate him. I'm angry, yes, that he'd been plotting against us while pretending to be our friend. Yet he'd shown the sort of bravery and cunning too that I can't help but admire. And you can't choose your parents, can you? I know that, as well as anyone.

Up ahead, the grey horse turns left towards Paris. Just before we carry on out of sight, Sebastien turns in his saddle.

'I'm sorry!' he calls out.

I nod: so am I.

Back in Annonay, we're welcomed home like conquering heroes. The sounds of cheering and festival music greet us before we've even crossed the river. As we hit the town itself, people line the streets and lean out of upstairs windows, waving anything they can get their hands on that's red, gold or blue. Somewhere in all of this I feel like I belong, like I've a right to call this town my home.

*

At the house, I reclaim my little bedroom with the painted white floor. It's decided that Coco should sleep outside from now on, on account of his crowing, which starts at two o'clock each morning and lasts until sunrise, without fail. Though I still tend the animals in the morning, in the afternoons Pierre is teaching me to read and write. Madame Verte and Odette get used to this new arrangement: I'm just another Montgolfier to feed and bathe and roll their eyes at when they think no one's looking.

But, like ropes dangling from the balloon, there are still some things I can't always get a hold of. Like why life seems so much harder when you're a girl. As I learn my letters in this same house where Camille was forbidden to learn hers, I think of all that might've been different if she'd been allowed to grow into a decent person, rather than being pitted against everyone else.

Meanwhile, Monsieur Joseph and Monsieur Etienne are working on their next prototype, one that will this time very publicly carry humans not animals. Monsieur de Rozier, the science man, is to be the first passenger.

A man.

I wonder if any of them realize that that none of this would've happened without women. Strange, I know, but true. It took Camille to get me into the

Montgolfiers' house. Madame Montgolfier's under-garments to solve the hot air mystery. Even Lancelot played her part in buying us a bit of time. And I like to think that I had something to do with it all, too.

That autumn, after months of huffing and puffing and complaining of backache, Madame Montgolfier gives birth to a baby girl. She's the most perfect little thing in the world, though don't tell Coco I said so.

One sleepy Sunday, not long after she's born, we're gathered around the fire in the salon, marvelling at our newest Montgolfier. As she still doesn't have a first name, we all agree it's time to put that right.

'She should have a strong name,' Monsieur Joseph says. 'Something serious and scholarly. We need to do better by our womenfolk in this family.'

I'm glad to hear it.

'Perhaps we could call her Camille?' Monsieur Etienne suggests.

I must've pulled a face because Pierre laughs. 'I'm not sure that's the best idea, uncle, all things considered.'

'Quite,' Monsieur Joseph agrees. 'We're looking to the future, not the past.'

'In which case, I'd like Magpie to name her,' Madame Montgolfier says, to my surprise. 'You're her big sister, so I think you should.'

I'm flattered, I really am. Though Pierre's got a glint of mischief in his eye. 'Without wishing to be funny, Magpie, your parents weren't exactly experts on names.'

'I don't honestly know who named me,' I admit. That's all I say though: I don't mention how in my thieving days it fitted me well. That's my secret never to be told.

'Well, I have to say it suits you,' Pierre remarks.

Alarmed, I catch his eye. An understanding passes between us. And that's the moment I realize: he knows exactly who I am. He always has done. He knows I'm the girl who broke into his house to steal the box, and all this time, he's told no one, not even me. I feel the panic start. Then, amazingly, a new sort of calm. Because it means Pierre knows all of me, doesn't it, not just the good bits. And we're still the very best of friends.

'Go on, *cherie*,' Madame Montgolfier passes the baby to me. 'What name do you think would suit her?'

Looking down at the sleeping bundle in my arms, I rack my brains. My sister is a Montgolfier; she deserves a decent first name to go with it. Pierre and his mother are waiting for me to say something.

'I'm sorry, I'll have to think about it,' I say, eventually.

In my arms, I feel a little wriggle. My sister stretches her legs, rubs her eyes with tiny fists and yawns.

'Hello, Sleepy.' I plant a kiss on her nose.

She wakes properly then, blinking up at me. Out of nowhere, the name slides into my head.

'Ariel,' I say out loud. 'We'll call her Ariel.'

'Ariel Montgolfier,' Pierre mulls it over. 'Hmmm. I like it, though isn't Ariel more of a boy's name?

'Says who?' Madame Montgolfier insists. 'If Magpie thinks it's right then it's perfect.'

And it is, because her eyes are the colour of my favourite type of sky – blue, with not a hint of cloud. My sister, I decide, is going to grow up brave and clever and I won't let anyone tell her otherwise. This Montgolfier girl is going to fly.

ABOUT THE BOOK

The Montgolfier hot-air balloon, a magnificent blue orb with dashes of gold, decorated with signs of the zodiac and multiple suns, was unveiled before King Louis XVI of France and his court at the royal palace of Versailles in September 1793.

The wonder of its age — an invention of significance, as it promised military advantage over France's old enemy, England — was the pride of the nation. Not only were the King and his courtiers in attendance, but so were the 'common people', there to witness a scientific and technological marvel.

Some say the balloon's passengers were chosen to replace the Montgolfier brothers, as the inaugural flight was seen as too dangerous to risk its brilliant inventors' lives. Others say that the passengers were selected on scientific grounds: a bird that could fly, a bird that could not, and an animal never expected to leave the security of terra firma.

Amazing as it might sound, implausible as it may appear, on that bright autumnal day, as the balloon was untethered and began its ascent into the sky, a duck, a rooster and a sheep became the first creatures sent to the heavens by man — and therefore became the first aeronauts.

Neal Jackson, winner of The Big Idea Competition. London, 2017.

ACKNOWLEDGEMENTS

First thanks goes to Neal Jackson, whose eye for good story potential won him The Big Idea Competition back in 2014. Huge thanks also to the Chicken House team – Barry, Rachel H, Rachel L, Jazz, Kes, Elinor, Laura – for asking me to create a story from Neal's idea, and then waiting patiently for me to do so! The flight was delayed due to brain fog – I'm so sorry – but here's hoping the take off will be smooth. I'd like to thank David Litchfield for his stunning cover. It's an absolute honour to have his artwork on the book. Lastly, my gratitude as always to The Muse, history itself, for offering up some real gems that allowed my imagination to take flight.

the big idea
competition

Have you got a great idea for a children's story?

Win a chance of seeing your idea transformed into a story for children.

- Written by a well-known children's author
- Championed by a top publisher and entertainment experts
- Published worldwide
- Made into a movie, TV, theatre, or more . . .

Go to thebigideacompetition.co.uk
Closing date for entries:
23rd February 2018